Contents

List of Characters 7
Prologue 9
1 Crazy Cloudburst 11
2 Duck and Cover 19
3 Oak Glen Gathering 31
4 Dust Devil Danger 43
5 Sturtevant Falls 53
6 Luke's Lion Farm 63
7 Ferocious Football 71
8 Knott's Berry Farm 81
9 Gravel Gertie's Flood 95
10 The California Alligator Farm 103
11 Lightning Strike 113
12 Hawk's Harvest Party 123
Epilogue 133
Carol Ann's Photo Album 134
For More Information 139
Recipe Card 141
Glossary 143
Preview 147

■ 5 ■

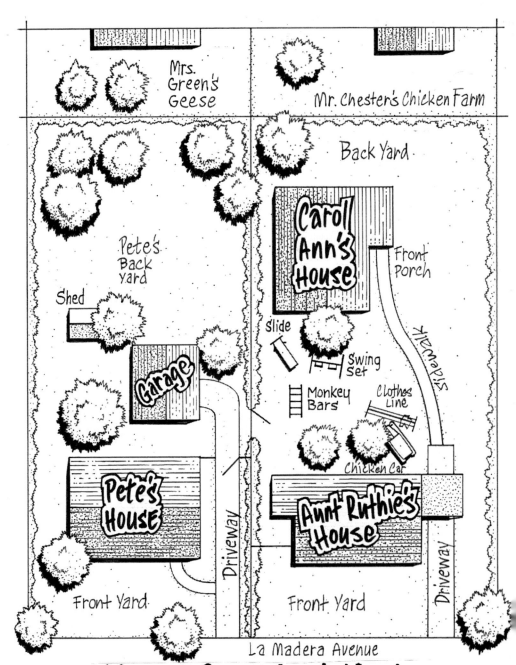

LIST OF CHARACTERS

THE HARTNELLS:
Carol Ann, age 11
Kathleen, age 9 (Younger Sister)
Gail, age 7 (Youngest Sister)
Mark (Baby Brother)
Jeanne (Mom)
Harry (Dad)
Granny Mary (Harry and Ruth's mom)

THE McCAMMONS:
Dr. Ruth (Aunt Ruthie)
Dr. Charles (Uncle Charlie)
Little Charlie, age 7 (Cousin)
Cathie, age 6 (Cousin)
Jimmie (Baby Cousin)

THE HAWKINGS:
Pete, age 11
John/Hawk, age 16 (Older Brother/Owner of 1937 Ford named Hawk's Ride)
Mary Jane, age 12/13 (Older Sister)
Mandy, age 7 (Younger Sister)
Pete's Mom

HAWK'S FRIENDS:
Ernie, age 16 (Owner of 1932 Ford hot rod named Wild Panther)
Tim, age 16 (Polio Survivor)

CHICAGO RELATIVES:
Granny Catherine Biehl (Jeanne's Mom)
Great Aunt Julie Cummins (Granny Catherine's Sister)
Great Uncle Wilson Cummins (Great Aunt Julie's Husband)

NEIGHBORS:
Mr. Chester (Chicken Farmer on property behind the Hartnells)
The Cruisers and Surfers
School and Church Friends

Prologue

Sturtevant Falls

The city of El Monte is located in the San Gabriel Valley of Southern California. It's a principal valley in California east of Los Angeles and south of the San Gabriel Mountain range. The valley got its name from the San Gabriel River that flows through it to the Pacific Ocean. During the 1950s, the valley was a farming community.

Most of the year, the San Gabriel Valley enjoys a warm, sunny Mediterranean-type climate. During the month of October, the average high temperature is 83 degrees with a low of 55 degrees. Dirt twisters, called dust devils, spiral up in farmer's fields or on dusty playgrounds. The valley's weather can range from smoggy, to snowy, to windy, and at times to rainy.

California is a land of little rain, but some years it gets a lot of wet weather which makes it prone to flooding. The Los Angeles Flood of 1938 was the area's most famous flood. Heavy rainfall in the mountains sent debris flowing down its canyons and into the San Gabriel River.

In later years, flash floods caused by wild weather flowed across the valley and affected the massive housing boom in El Monte and the surrounding area. Pete and Carol Ann experienced many wild weather conditions that October of 1955.

1

Crazy Cloudburst

The thunder roared with a *RUMBLE, CRACKLE,* and *BOOM* like a great, grouchy voice in the sky. From the top of the slide, I looked at the dark clouds overhead. Cold raindrops pelted me like icy darts. A zigzag of lightning flashed across the sky followed by explosive sounds. *Yikes.*

My ten-month-old beagle puppy barked at the booming noises while waiting for me at the bottom of the slide. I let go of the railing and zoomed like lightning down into a mud puddle. A wave of brown water splashed Buddy causing him to scoot back. Torrential raindrops pounded the slide like a drum.

"Let's go, Buddy," I said and waved my arm. "We're in danger next to this metal slide! It could attract a bolt of lightning and fry us like crispy critters."

"Hurry up, Carol Ann!" yelled my good friend, Pete, as he herded the little kids under the carport on the back of my Aunt Ruthie's house. Pete and the kids huddled together in their soaking wet clothes like a group of soaked scarecrows.

I pulled the neck of my sweater over my head and dashed past Mom's clothesline, past the chicken car, and up the slick sidewalk. Buddy and I pattered through puddles and ducked under the wooden carport while rain swirled around us. Raindrops beat the roof above our heads like a million falling pebbles.

I snuggled next to Kathleen and Gail, my two younger sisters. Our cousins, Little Charlie and Cathie, held each other while eleven-year-old Pete hugged his younger sister, Mandy. Instead of snuggling with us, Buddy shook his tan, white, and black body. He reminded me of one of Mom's mixer beaters. His long, droopy ears whipped back and forth and sprayed muddy water everywhere.

Dirty mud spots dotted Pete's plaid shirt and the little kids' faces with brown polka dots. "Hey, Buddy," said Pete, "You're muddy and now we are, too."

"Hey, Buddy," said my seven-year-old sister, Gail. "You muddied me all over." Gail wiped her face. The puppy looked up at her and woofed.

Pete pointed and said, "Look at that hen go!" A mother hen flitted towards us on the sidewalk with her wings out over her chicks. She rushed them under our chicken car. "That hen ducked to safety just like we did."

"She's a smart chicken to escape from Mr. Chester's yard and live here in our yard. Thankfully, Mr. Chester got tired of chasing Buddy the beagle hound around his backyard, and he gave him to me."

Buddy wagged his white-tipped tail and howled with a wailing sound that competed with the pounding rain.

More thunder *CRACKLED and BOOMED* as lightning flashed across the dark, sinister sky. The little kids whimpered like scared puppies. *I want to whimper, too, but I need to be brave even though the thunder and lightning are making my teeth chatter.*

"The storm is overhead right now," said Pete. "It's boss that we're studying weather in our science class at school. Clouds have cool Latin names. Those are nimbus clouds above us dumping out their rain. When you hear the thunder and see the lightning at the same time the storm is over your head."

We all looked up and waited for more scary sounds and frightening lightning. Another fiery bolt zigzagged across the distant sky and nearer the San Gabriel Mountains. Minutes later, we heard a faint booming and crackling.

Pete said, "Like crazy, like wow! The crazy cloudburst is over."

My nine-year-old sister, Kathleen, asked, "What's a crazy cloudburst?"

Pete said, "That's when the rain pours really fast and really hard out of the clouds and without any warning. A cloudburst can have lightning, too, like we just saw all around us. Usually, it only lasts a few minutes, but it dumps out so much rain it can cause floods."

"Pete's right," I said. "I looked up Bible verses about weather and wrote them down because we're studying it." I pulled my dry three-inch by five-inch red, spiral-sided notepad from my pocket, flipped several lined pages, and read, "Psalm 97:4 says, 'His lightnings lit up the world; the earth saw and trembled.' Just now, the lightning from the cumulus nimbus clouds made us tremble."

"You're so cool to write down Bible verses and share them with us," said Pete. "By the way, cumulus nimbus clouds are dark clouds filled with rain and piled on top of each other."

"Carol Ann is a cool writer . . . er," said seven-year-old Gail as she smiled up at me.

Seven-year-old Little Charlie asked, "What is lightning?"

"It's a flash of light in the sky caused by an electric current," I answered.

"Yeah," said Pete. "It's a spark that flashes between clouds or from clouds to earth. And clouds form from condensed water vapor in cool air."

Behind us, the screen door going into Aunt Ruthie's kitchen squeaked open and revealed Granny Mary standing there. Six-year-old cousin Cathie rushed over to our grandmother like a lightning bolt and buried her face in Granny Mary's printed apron.

"Inside," said my grandmother as she motioned us into the house. "Eat cookies," she said in her hard-to-understand Russian accent. *Granny Mary immigrated to America from Latvia before I was born.*

"Cookies!" exclaimed Pete as he pushed the kids through the door into the warm, welcoming kitchen that smelled like brown sugar and molasses. *Pete loves cookies.*

Before Pete could herd me into the house, I bent down to Buddy's eye level and said, "You stay out here, Buddy, and I'll bring you a doggy treat." Buddy, the hound dog, danced in a circle then sat down on the door mat to wait for his treat.

Our soaked and straggly gang sat around the kitchen table and eyeballed a trayful of treats. We greedily reached for Mom's home-baked Munch Mouth Molasses Cookies.

"Eat," said Granny Mary as she washed dishes at the kitchen sink.

Pete bit into a sugar-covered cookie and said, "Like wow!"

"Yum," I said as I bit into one of Mom's molasses cookies. "Mom baked these this morning and brought them over to Aunt Ruthie's house for our afterschool snack." *I'm glad we live behind Aunt Ruthie's house, so it's a quick walk on the sidewalk for Mom to deliver cookies.* Pete's the Munch Mouth of La Madera Avenue.

Little Charlie said, "Auntie Jeanne makes the *bestest* cookies." I smiled in agreement for Mom's *bestest* cookies.

"I helped Mommy bake them," said Gail. "I stirred up the dog."

"Gail, you stirred up the dough not the dog," said Kathleen. *Poor Kathleen spends a load of time correcting poor Gail who gets a lot of words mixed up.*

Soon, nothing but crumbs remained. Seven-year-old Mandy leaned next to Pete. He brushed her wet, blonde hair out of her eyes. *Mom says Pete and Mandy spend more time here than at their house next door. That's fine, because Pete is my "bestest" friend.*

More rain plinked against the kitchen window. "That crazy cloudburst isn't done doing crazy things," I said as we cleaned up then departed the kitchen for the living room.

The kids scrambled to the game cupboard as Pete and I sat down near the roaring fire in the fireplace. Soon, Mr. Potato Head and paper dolls littered the braided rug.

Pete asked, "Did you write your weather essay for class?"

I nodded my head up and down and said, "I started writing my essay about lightning, and today I got to see some. It was scary but real cool, too. Last night I looked up lightning in our "L" encyclopedia. Now I can add firsthand experience."

"I looked up flash floods in our encyclopedia set," said Pete. "Did you know the Los Angeles Flood of 1938 killed over a hundred people and flooded the whole San Gabriel Valley . . . right where we live? Muddy, debris-filled water destroyed a man's house and washed him down the mountain in his bathtub. He broke both his legs. The flood waters and mud roared off of the San Gabriel Mountains like hopped-up hot rods."

"Wow, I didn't know that," I said. "That must have been very scary. Everyone's essays are due on Tuesday, October fourth. I can't wait to hear you read your essay out loud in front of the class."

"Yeah, I *really* can't wait to read my essay out loud . . . in front of the whole class," said Pete sarcastically.

"I'm scared to stand up in front of the class and read out loud," I admitted. "I hope those three bully boys in our class don't make fun of me. Maybe the *Duck and Cover* movie we're watching that day will take too long, so we won't have to read our essays after all."

"Fat chance of that happening," said Pete. "We saw that flick last year, and it didn't take very long. Do you remember how the song goes? That turtle sings it like this: 'Dum Dum, Deedle Dum Dum, Deedle Dum Dum, Deedle Dum Dum' and so on."

"I remember that song," I said. "Luckily, we never had to do one of those *real* "Duck and Cover" drills. I hope I know what to do if an atom bomb ever dropped on us."

"If we hear a big boom, we need to drop, duck, and cover," said Pete.

BOOM, BOOM, CRACKLE, RUMBLE, BOOM, roared over the top of Aunt Ruthie's house. Buddy howled in a high, distressed tone from outside. Pete fell down, curled into a ball, and ducked his head under his arms. When lightning flashed and more thunder boomed in the distance, Pete peeked out of his "shell" and looked up at me.

"That was thunder, Pete," I said and held in a laugh. "It wasn't an atomic blast."

Pete stood up, brushed off his dusty jeans, smiled really big, and said, "I hear ya, Carol Ann. We were talking about duck and cover. That BOOM sent me to the floor. Ha, ha."

I laughed and said, "It's okay, Pete. I'm glad to see you remembered what to do. Listen to the rain. Do you think acid rain from an atom bomb sounds like this?"

"I don't know, and I don't want to know," answered Pete.

"Pete . . . eee!" yelled a girl's voice from outside in the front yard. Pete's older sister, Mary Jane, passed by the plate glass window. Her opened pink umbrella pulled her towards my aunt's porch like a parachute. When the doorbell rang its tune, the kids swiveled their heads like baby owls to look at the door.

"Someone open the door!" yelled Little Charlie from where he sat knee deep in Mr. Potato Head parts.

I got up, avoided the toys littering the floor, and opened the door. Thirteen-year-old Mary Jane stood there in her pink rain coat holding her folded, pink umbrella. One of her mud-splashed rain boots tapped impatiently on the concrete porch.

"Where's Pete and Mandy?" she snarled in an acid tone that

would vaporize acid rain. *Why worry about acid rain when Mary Jane lives next door?* I thought and smiled.

"Here I am," said Pete as he appeared next to me holding Mandy's hand. "Don't go ape on us, Sis. Control your temper."

"Hurry up," said Mary Jane. "Mom sent me outside in torrential rain to find you two. Hawk's waiting in his car to drive us over to Grandpa's house for the evening."

"Hold your horses, and cool it," said Pete. "We're right behind you. Let Mandy share your umbrella. I'm not afraid of a little cloudburst, so lead the way."

"What *little* cloudburst?" asked Mary Jane as she popped open her pink umbrella and ushered Mandy into the rain. Mary Jane gave me a dirty look before she cut out across the front yard. She mumbled to Mandy, "Carol Ann is bad news."

Pete waved goodbye and said, "See ya later, alligator, and you're not bad news."

"After while, crocodile," I said as I followed Pete onto the porch. He shoved his baseball cap onto his head, sprinted into the rain, and ducked into his yard next door. Pete's sixteen-year-old brother, handsome John "Hawk" Hawking, climbed out of his 1937 Ford, two-door Sedan with a slantback. The hot rod rumbled like thunder on their driveway.

Pete followed Mary Jane and Mandy into the backseat of the red-orange car called Hawk's Ride. Pete's brother waved to me then ducked inside his car to avoid the water that streamed across the car's chopped top and flowed over the painted flames on the car's hood and sides.

Pete says it's cherry and the coolest machine at El Monte High School. I agree. Hawk's friends had helped him create the car's chopped top. Pete told me the teens had cut the top off, chopped down the window walls, and welded the top back onto the car.

VROOM, VROOM, roared Hawk's Ride as it rumbled down the

driveway to La Madera Avenue. Hawk stopped at the end of his driveway to avoid hitting a black Chevy pickup truck that cruised by on the street. *That's a cherry machine, too,* I thought.

I went back into the house as another blast of thunder boomed far away. *Pete's essay about the ferocious Los Angeles Flood of 1938 sounds really scary. Did the 1938 Flood happen after a crazy cloudburst like today? Could it happen again? Yikes.*

At Uncle Charlie's bookcase, I pulled down his giant Bible Concordance filled with Bible verses. *I'll look up more verses about the weather and write them in my little, red, spiral-sided notepad here in my pocket. I also need to look up verses about having wisdom to make wise choices in scary situations.*

I turned the pages of the concordance and found the Bible verse I needed that I could share with Pete. I wrote down Timothy 1:7. 'For God hath not given us a spirit of fear; but of power, and of love, and of a sound mind.' *No matter what happens, I need to remember this and believe it.*

Now, only sprinkles pitter-patted on the windows. *I don't know if there's anything in the Bible about sprinkles, but I do know there's a flood story about Noah, his family, and lots of animals. Will today's crazy cloudburst cause The Great October Flood of 1955?*

2

Duck and Cover

VROOM, VROOM, VROOM, roared Hawk's Ride next to us as Pete and I kicked stones across La Madera Avenue on our way to Cherrylee School. When the car rolled to a stop, Hawk's friend, Tim, rolled down the hot rod's passenger side window.

"Hawk wants to know if you kids want a lift to school?" asked Tim.

"Thanks, but no thanks," said Pete. "We like walking, so we can kick rocks and stuff all the way to school. Plus, we're meeting our friends on the way. See ya."

"That's cool, Kid," said Pete's brother from the driver's seat. "Have a blast today and stay out of trouble." With a roar, the car sped off towards El Monte High School.

"What trouble is Hawk talking about?" I asked Pete.

"Awe, it's nothing I can't handle," said Pete. "That big bully, Rex, tried to pick a fight with me on the playground yesterday. I stood up to him, and he didn't like it."

"I missed that. What if red-haired Rex picks a fight with you today?" I asked with concern as I kicked an asphalt chunk across the street and under the parked Chevy pickup I saw during the crazy cloudburst.

"If he does, I'll duck and cover," laughed Pete as we turned the corner onto The Wye. "Did you see the *El Monte Herald* newspaper this morning?"

■ 19 ■

"No," I said. "I only look at it when we need to do current events."

"On the front page, Mom read me an article about three youths who were arrested for stealing a jacket from the outlet store on Valley Boulevard," said Pete. "The paper didn't mention their names, but they could be the three bullies in our class."

"I wonder if they'll be in class today," I said as the Bailey brothers met us. "And by the way, I wrote down a good Bible verse for you whenever you feel the urge to duck and cover." I patted my pocket which contained my notepad and stubby pencil.

We approached Cherrylee's beige, Art Deco-style buildings on a horseshoe-shaped lot where The Wye split into two different streets. Colorful fall leaves fluttered down from several tall trees and littered the grassy area in front of the school. Old leaves crunched underfoot as we stepped along the sidewalk past the office.

Inside our sixth-grade classroom, I sat down at my desk near the front of the room. Our teacher, Mrs. Rose, wrote Tuesday, October 4, 1955 in white chalk on the blackboard then listed our assignments for the day.

After taking attendance, Mrs. Rose said, "Please stand and recite The Pledge of Allegiance with me." Our chairs scraped on the linoleum floor as we stood up and placed our hands over our hearts.

"I pledge allegiance to the flag of the United States of America and to the Republic for which it stands, one nation under God, indivisible, with liberty and justice for all." We sat back down with more scraping sounds and began our school day.

"Class, this morning we will watch, then discuss, a very important movie," explained Mrs. Rose as she readied the projector. "Many of you have seen it before. The movie is called *Duck and Cover*. Pete, will you please turn off the lights."

The movie flickered on the classroom movie screen. A cartoon character named Bert the Turtle plodded down a tree-lined street singing the same song Pete sang the other day. "Dum Dum, Deedle Dum Dum, Deedle Dum Dum, Deedle Dum Dum."

The narrator said, "When danger threatened him he never got hurt, he knew just what to do. There was a turtle by the name of Bert, and Bert the Turtle was very alert. He'd duck and cover. Duck and cover. He did what we all must learn to do. You and you and you and you. Duck and cover."

In the movie, Bert wore a pith helmet and black bow tie. As he plodded along smelling a flower in his hand, an evil-looking monkey sitting in a tree threatened Bert by dangling a sizzling firecracker before him. Bert the Turtle ducked into his shell as the firecracker exploded. The bad cartoon monkey disappeared.

Then a man's voice said, "That's what this film is all about, 'Duck and Cover.'"

For the next six minutes, our sixth grade class at Cherrylee School watched the movie called *Duck and Cover*. I shivered with goose bumps as we saw actual atomic blasts, real people running for cover, and cars trying to leave the city. Kids like us in a classroom listened to their teacher one minute then ducked under their desks the next. *Yikes, that could happen to us!* I thought. *But God doesn't give us a spirit of fear.*

"If you see the bright light," said the narrator, "you'll have one to thirty seconds to protect yourself from flying debris and heat. If you don't see the light, you were killed."

The film showed a blast ripping through buildings and making them collapse into rubble. *Oh, dear, I never want to see a blast, or a flash, or a mushroom cloud, or a collapsing building. I saw this movie in fifth grade, but I forgot most of it!* I glanced around the classroom at the other kids. They grimaced and gasped and squirmed and frowned and fretted just like I did.

"An atomic blast can knock you down," warned the friendly narrator. "It can also give you a sunburn." In the film, a boy jumped off his bicycle and dived into a ditch. The narrator continued, "A newspaper or cloth could give protection. We must be ready for an attack just as we are ready for many other dangers that are all around us."

"Stay away from windows," Bert said, "because they may break and cut you."

I'm sure glad I sit near the wall and away from the windows. But Pete and his friends are by windows that could break and cut them. Ouch.

Phrases like "getting ready," "the bomb," "bright light," "atomic flash," "when the bomb goes off," "duck and cover," "the enemy," "anytime, anywhere," and "nuclear attack" exploded like flashes in my mind.

"Sundays, holidays, vacation-time, any time, we must always be ready for the atom bomb," said the narrator. "We must do the right thing when the atom bomb goes off . . . duck and cover!" When the film ended, the whole class sighed in relief along with the bully boys who sat in the back of the room. *They're here, so they didn't get arrested.*

Mrs. Rose turned off the projector. Her high heels *click, click, clicked* across the floor as she went to the front of the class. "Lights please," she said. Eileen jumped up to turn them on. "Thank you, Eileen, and thank you, Class, for your quiet attention."

After we watched this scary film last year, Pete sang Bert's song for weeks, I thought. *Some kids called him Pete the Turtle. They said he sang worse than an A-bomb explosion. He didn't like that, so he stopped singing, "Dum Dum, Deedle Dum Dum."*

Mrs. Rose held up a booklet and said, "This is a teaching guide issued by the F.C.D.A. Does anyone know what those letters stand for?"

"They stand for Federal Civil Defense Administration," said Wilbur, the smartest kid in our class. Soft snickering sounded in the background.

"Thank you, Wilbur," said Mrs. Rose. "In 1950, the United States Congress established the F.C.D.A. to educate and protect our citizens. They made this film for school children. Becky, will you please pass out these pamphlets. The film demonstrates basic principles of self-protection in case of a nuclear explosion. Are there any questions?"

Hands shot up around the classroom like stalks in a Kansas cornfield. My "stalk" stayed on my desk. *What about fallout, flashes, and food stockpiles? Like a goof, I'm too scared to ask questions. Will I remember what to do in a real blast?*

Pete asked a question, "Who is the enemy that the flick is talking about? Is it the Reds?" The whole class eyeballed Pete.

"They're called Communists, Mr. Hawking, and we're not discussing them today," answered our teacher.

As hands continued to shoot up, questions and answers swirled around me like ripples in a river. I flipped through the pamphlet. It overflowed with information or *illuminations*, as Pete would say, to put us in orbit . . . in the know. The lunch bell rang with a loud and long ringing sound.

Mrs. Rose stopped the lunch migration with her outstretched hand. "One minute, please," she said. "After lunch, be prepared to read your essays. And remember, we'll probably have a Civil Defense Drill sometime soon. So please be ready."

Lunch in the Cherrylee cafetorium turned into its usual war of words. Each group of kids topped the next group's volume. The teacher who monitored lunch patiently strolled around discouraging the noise. Her shrill whistle warned us of serious consequences for bad behavior. That didn't stop Rex, the bully, from bopping one poor kid on the head. *Ouch.*

My peanut butter sandwich, chips, and apple tasted yummy. Pete eyeballed my two cookies and said with a smile, "Hmmm, you know, Carol Ann, if we have an atomic blast right now, you won't have time to eat both chocolate chip cookies."

"That's not funny, Pete," I said with a frown. "But like a good friend, I'll share."

"Mmm . . . m," said Pete as he bit into my extra cookie. "Thanks, Carol Ann. You're mom's the best cookie-baker." He smacked his lips, licked crumbs from the corners, and motioned to the Bailey brothers. "Let's split." They paraded out to the playground, while their comments about the *Duck and Cover* movie echoed back to me.

"That movie told us a lot of bad news," said one of the Bailey boys.

"I thought a blast meant to have a good time not a nuclear explosion," said Pete.

"What a boss flick," said another boy. "Bert the Turtle fractured me."

"Yeah, me too," said Pete. "My dad says we need to pound those Reds."

Becky, Susan, Eileen, and I pounded a ball in a game of Foursquare. A breeze teased my hair and cooled my sweaty face as I retrieved the ball for the tenth time.

Eileen served the ball to me. She said, "My dad read an article in the newspaper about Area D Civil Defense needing volunteers to operate their radios and rescue trucks. He has first aid training, so he volunteered to drive the Civil Defense Rescue Truck."

Eileen slapped the foursquare ball to Becky who said, "My mom is good at math, so she volunteered to drive the Radio Activity Survey Truck."

"My mom read me the article about Dr. and Mrs. R. P. Shuler who celebrated their fiftieth wedding anniversary," said Eileen. "My folks know them and their children. The newspaper called them 'A Real American Family.'"

Susan swatted the ball and squealed, "Are you girls ready to read your essays today? I hope I don't faint. That would be so uncool. I'd feel like a real goof."

Our heads bobbed up and down in agreement to the rhythm of the bouncing foursquare ball. When the bell rang, we tramped back to class to face our awful assignments.

Susan said, "I wrote about the frost that affects the orange groves surrounding my Aunt Shirley's house in the city of *Corona* which means 'crown.' Grand Avenue circles Corona, so it's called The Circle City."

"I wrote about rain," said Eileen. "An orange grove in Corona would be fun to visit even if they do get frost."

"I wrote about the snow that falls in our local mountains," chimed in Becky as we neared our classroom.

Back in class, papers rattled in nervous fingers. Kids readied their weather essays to read out loud. I shuffled my essay and worried. *Why is it so difficult to stand up in class and read some paragraphs out loud? It only takes a few seconds. I know why. In those few seconds, a kid might make a mistake, and the class will laugh.*

"Pssssssstttt," Pete hissed at me in a whisper. He gave me a thumbs-up sign and mouthed the words "made in the shade." *I'm sure glad Pete believes in me when I don't.*

"Thanks," I mouthed. *Last year in fifth grade, Henry Gomez read out loud and burped in the middle of a sentence. One loud, bubbly burp and the class had dissolved into laughter. Henry's face had beamed bright red like a stop light.*

Afterward, Pete had whispered, "That gas cooked."

Anything can happen during a speech, I thought. *I hope anything won't happen today during my speech. Da dump* pounded my heart. I pulled my notepad from my pocket, flipped some pages, and read to myself. *Joshua 1:9 says, 'Be strong and of good courage.'* Below it, I read from John 14:27, *'Peace I leave with you . . . Let not your heart be troubled, neither let it be afraid.'* I took a deep, calming breath.

The A's thru F's shared their weather essays: a drive through fog, wild waves at Huntington Beach, a heat wave in San Diego, and horrible, hot Santa Ana winds blowing through the Mission Inn out in Riverside. I glanced one more time at my notepad and read from Proverbs 2:6. *'For the LORD giveth wisdom . . .' and power,* I thought.

Mrs. Rose clapped her hands. "What fine essays. Now, Henry, it's your turn."

The class rustled in anticipation as Henry stood up. *Could a kid have two back-to-back accidents, one year apart, and in a different classroom?* Henry Gomez got ready to read while we waited. His essay about tornadoes didn't have any burps. Henry finished reading and sat down. *I'm next. Yikes.*

"What is your essay about, Carol Ann?" asked Mrs. Rose.

I wiggled out of my chair and stood up. With nervous fingers, I picked up my paper. My heart pounded. *Breathe in . . . breathe out,* I told myself. *I'm wise, courageous, and at peace . . . sort of. Plus, I don't have a spirit of fear . . . but of power.*

"My weather essay is about lightning," I read, "It happens . . . when . . . ."

An ear-splitting, head-pounding, wailing noise shook the walls of our classroom. *What is this awful noise?*

"DROP!" yelled Mrs. Rose.

Down I dropped onto the cold floor and scooted under my desk. I tucked my head into my knees then held my hands over my neck. *Duck and cover, duck and cover,* I rehearsed in my mind. *Can a newspaper protect me from radiation?*

During the movie, didn't Bert say, "Remember what to do, friends? Now tell me right out loud. What are you supposed to do when you see the flash?" Did I see a flash before I dropped under my desk? Yikes.

My forehead rested on the floor that smelled like bleach and chemicals. My limbs shook, and goose bumps covered my skin. *At least I can still feel, but for how much longer? Will fallout invade my lungs and choke me? How long will it take for radiation or acid rain from an atom bomb to seep into our classroom?* My teeth chattered like ice in a glass.

The siren continued its eerie, wild wailing.

Someone burped, but no one laughed. My speech forgotten, I prayed and listened. Classmates around me breathed loudly, shuffled softly, and whimpered weakly.

I whispered, "O God, give us peace, power, and wisdom like you said you would. And, please, keep us safe."

The screeching siren stopped. Our normally noisy classroom seemed curiously quiet except for loud breathing. *Are we safe? Did part of the school blow up?*

"You can get up, Class," said Mrs. Rose. "I'm so proud of you. You did an excellent job of ducking and covering."

I crawled like a slug into my seat and looked around. Mrs. Rose straightened her navy suit. I brushed lint and fuzz from my skirt. I gulped in a deep breath as my shaking fingers fumbled through my brown hair. I tucked a stray strand behind my ear. Many kids looked dazed. *If I get really lucky, they won't pay any attention to me if I still have to read my essay.*

"Carol Ann," said Mrs. Rose, "you may read your essay about lightning now."

Oh, those dreaded words. *O God, help me, please,* I prayed, gulped, stood up on rubbery legs, and read my essay. When I finished reading, I looked up from my paper. I sat down and exhaled in relief. *Yea! I did it.* Pete gave me a thumbs-up.

When the end-of-school-bell rang, half the class jumped in their seats. Pete played it off like he wasn't scared, but I saw him lift off his seat, too. I looked over at Rex and his friends, Stu and

Neil. They looked like trouble as they left their chairs with smirks on their faces. *What trouble will they cause outside our classroom?*

In front of Cherrylee School, kids streamed out of the buildings like ants at an October picnic. The trees surrounding the school shook in the afternoon breeze as leaves fell around us. We took off down The Wye kicking gravel bits that crumbled at the edge of the road. The gravel skittered into piles of fall leaves.

"How'd you like the duck and cover drill?" Pete asked. "Wasn't it unreal?"

"I hated it," I said. "That drill seemed too real and too scary."

"I knew it had to be a drill. My dad said President Eisenhower is doing everything he can to stay in a cold war and to stop another hot war," said Pete.

"My dad said the same thing. He's hoping the cold war doesn't heat up."

"Did you know that last Friday there was an air raid siren alert test?" asked Pete.

"Yes," I said, "Mom warned me about it. It blasted really loud, because the main siren is mounted on an old El Monte fire station."

Pete cocked his head sideways and asked a question, "Uh, why didn't you jump right up when the drill ended? You stayed on your hands and knees for a long time. What were you doing? Praying?"

I stopped and kicked a big asphalt chunk. "Yep," I said. "Prayer seemed like a good idea. While I waited on my knees during that scary drill, I heard kids sniffling. So I asked God to help us and to protect us."

"You're so hip, Carol Ann." Pete laughed. "Only you would pray when we're on our hands and knees during a duck and cover drill."

"I'm sure I wasn't the only one praying," I said.

Rex, Neil, and Stu surrounded us. Rex mimicked Pete, "You're so hip, Carol Ann." Rex continued contemptuously, "Only you would pray when we're on our hands and knees during a duck and cover drill."

"Will you pray for us?" asked Neil in a scornful voice.

I stared at the three tough-looking boys and said, "Sure, I'll pray for you."

"Ha," laughed Rex as he elbowed his friends. "Is she for real? She wants to pray for us!"

"Knock it off," said Pete, "and leave Carol Ann alone. Aren't you guys late for a date or something?"

Pete didn't flinch as Rex sauntered up, leaned into him, and glared. Rex laughed. "This kid thinks he's as tough as his older brother, but he's not. I say he's a chicken. Let's split, Guys." They gushed up the street like a bad wind blowing hot air.

"Those guys are cruisin for a bruisin," said Pete.

"You're the hip one the way you handled those bullies," I said as we turned onto our street. "Those boys are scarier than reading my essay."

"They don't scare me," said Pete. "I was more scared to read my essay out loud. No kid likes to read out loud *or* get into a fistfight."

"I thought I'd get out of reading my essay because of the duck and cover drill," I said. "But I didn't get *that* lucky. At least I didn't burp or throw up or faint from fright. Oh, and I found a Bible verse for you from Timothy 1:7. It says, 'For God hath not given us a spirit of fear; but of power, and of love, and of a sound mind.'" *I need this, too.*

"Thanks for that good Bible verse," said Pete. Then he sang in a teasing voice, "Dum, dum, deedle dum dum, deedle dum dum."

"Not that," I begged as a wailing, siren-type sound split the afternoon calm.

FEROCIOUS FALL

"Duck and cover," Pete yelled as he dropped to the road, rolled into a ball, and covered his neck. He peeked out in time to see an ambulance drive by on Lower Azuza Road. "Oops, false alarm," he said as he jumped up.

"Well, Pete, you're ready for anything," I laughed and sang, "Remember what to do, friends. Now tell me right out loud. What are you supposed to do when you see the flash . . . of the ambulance?"

"Duck and cover," we sang together. "Duck and cover, duck and cover," echoed down La Madera Avenue. I thought, *Will I have to duck and cover from a Rex-bomb sometime in the future?*

3

Oak Glen Gathering

After almost two hours on the road, Hawk's Ride rumbled along the final stretch to the apple orchards in Oak Glen. We had traveled Route 66 to Waterman then on minor roads to the apple-picking paradise in the hills of San Bernardino.

Hawk and his friends sat on the front seat while Pete, Mary Jane, Mrs. Hawking, and I shared side-by-side space in the back. Mandy squirmed around on her mom's lap while Buddy rested on mine. He looked up at me and gave me an "Are we there yet?" look. *I'm wondering the same thing.*

On both sides of the uphill road, trees and bushes wore fall colors. Their leaves had changed from green to red, gold, and yellow because of the crisp, cold air at night. Cirrus clouds looked like wispy curls floating in the blue sky. Hawk revved his car as he drove by apple orchards and into the town of Oak Glen.

"I think we've arrived," said Pete. "Oak Glen looks the same as last year."

"Well, it's about time!" said Mary Jane. "Carol Ann's been hogging all the space on the back seat. I've been *squished* this whole ride."

"Lighten up, Sis," said Hawk. "You've been to Oak Glen before, so you know how long it takes to drive here. You could have gone to work with Dad at his auto parts shop. Then we wouldn't be *squished* by your constant complaining."

■ 31 ■

"That's enough, you two," said their mom. "We're almost to River Ranch Apple Orchard. We're *all* going to have fun picking apples. No more complaining, please."

Pete and I glanced over at Mary Jane to see how she took her mom's reprimand. A deep crease between her perfect brows meant trouble. She turned towards us, shrugged her shoulders, and stuck her tongue out between curled lips. Her blonde ringlets swung in Pete's face as she turned away from us.

Pete shrugged and moved his lips to say, "I'm sorry she's so spoiled."

Hawk's Ride rumbled past Law's Restaurant, several really quaint shops, and roadside apple stands. A crisp breeze blew through the car's open windows. *Maybe the breeze will cool off Mary Jane's hot temper.* Colorful trees lined the street and filled the distant park. Hawk drove up, up, up the road then zigzagged around curvy corners.

Out on a straightaway, Hawk slowed his car and turned right at a sign printed with big letters that spelled out RIVER RANCH. Across the road and next to us, fruit-covered apple trees displayed their bounty. *This is my first time in Oak Glen and I like it,* I thought.

"Yahoo, we're here," said Pete. "Now it's apple gathering time." Buddy howled his own form of yahoo.

"It sounds like Buddy wants to gather apples, too," I said as Hawk drove Hawk's Ride into a parking spot next to a grassy picnic area under lots of fall-colored trees.

Over by a wooden building, orange pumpkins cascaded from an upended wheelbarrow. Piles of pumpkins filled an antique wooden wagon. Cinnamon smells drifted through the open window to my nose. Buddy sniffed at the air, too.

"That's apple pie heaven over there in their bakery," said Pete. "I'm ready for a giant wedge of warm apple pie topped with heaps of homemade vanilla ice cream."

"After lunch, Son," said Pete's mom as she motioned for us to scoot out of the cramped car.

We popped out of Hawk's hot rod, gathered our picnic supplies, and migrated to the tables under the trees. More white, curly cirrus clouds sailed overhead while cold air shifted the red and gold leaves on the trees. Our teacher had informed us that *cirrus* was Latin for 'curls of hair.' I snuggled a little deeper into my warm sweater. Pete's mom placed a tin containing my mom's oatmeal cookies on a checkered tablecloth.

"Let's split and go pick apples, Carol Ann," said Pete as he pointed to the apple orchard. "Lunch won't be ready for a while. We can get buckets over there."

Pete and Buddy raced to the orchard. Buddy pulled me along behind him with the rope tied from his collar to my waist. The apples trees smelled sweet. Buddy's sensitive hound dog nose sniffed with a snuffling noise as we strolled between the rows of trees. Bees buzzed around the fruit that decorated branches like red Christmas ornaments.

"Did you know that apples are the most valuable fruit that grows on trees?" I asked Pete as I caught up with him.

"How do you know that?" Pete asked me.

"I looked up the word 'apple' in our encyclopedia set," I answered. "I also read that apples grow just about everywhere. And there are lots of apple stories."

"Only you would look up cool stuff about apples when you were gonna visit an apple orchard," said Pete as we progressed through the trees with the puppy leading us.

"Well, it's good to know something about a place you're going to visit," I said. "I learned about a real person named Johnny Appleseed."

"Aw gee, Carol Ann, wasn't he some kind of legend?" asked Pete.

"He was a real person, named John Chapman, who lived in the 1800s. He traveled all over Ohio and Indiana wearing a saucepan on his head, carrying his Bible and a bag of apple seeds. Everywhere he went he planted apple trees and shared the good news of the gospel." Buddy stopped snooping, looked up at me, and woofed.

"Wow! Johnny Appleseed must have been really brave," said Pete. Buddy seemed to agree about Johnny's bravery with more barking. Then he chased a flying insect.

"He *was* brave to work among the Indians and early settlers," I said.

We stopped at a huge apple tree with a rounded top and low-hanging branches covered in reddish fruit. Pete and I plucked apples and carefully placed them in our buckets. Buddy scurried around the base of the tree sniffing at fallen fruit while crunching leaves under his paws.

One row over from us, two workers picked apples. A man stood on a tall ladder leaning against a tree's trunk. Another man filled a cloth bag with the rosy-colored fruit. When he pulled a cord at the canvas bag's bottom, dozens of apples tumbled out like red balls into wooden boxes.

"Pete, my bucket's full of fruit," I said as I struggled to hold it up.

"Yeah, mine is too," said Pete. He reached up, plucked one more perfect, red apple from the tree next to him, and crunched his teeth through the apple's red "skin."

A few rows over, Mary Jane and Mandy stood by a tall, blond-haired farm boy. He wore blue denim overalls with a plaid, long-sleeved shirt. A straw hat shaded his face. He picked up Mandy and hoisted her up to pick apples. She giggled as she grabbed fruit. Buddy drooped his head sideways to listen.

Tall ladders leaned against several trees to access fruit on the top-most branches. The farm boy put Mandy down and climbed up one of the ladders. He picked fruit and put it into a bushel basket. Despite passing through dirt, grass, weeds and dusty branches, Mary Jane looked spotless in her jeans, pink plaid shirt, and pink sweater.

"Can't you pick those any faster?" she asked. "You're such a slow-poke. My neck's getting a kink in it from watching you."

"That's the last one," said the boy. He juggled the basket of apples with one arm, held onto the ladder with his free hand, and descended down to the ground.

"It's about time," said Mary Jane as she grabbed the dusty bushel basket of apples from the boy and stomped off. "Stay with me, Mandy, so you don't get lost."

The boy turned in our direction and said, "Hi, Pete and Carol Ann. What are you doing here in Oak Glen? That's a cute beagle hound."

"Hi, Stu," said Pete, as he blinked in surprise. "I didn't recognize you in your overalls and straw hat. What are *you* doing here?"

"My family drives here several times during the season," answered Stu. "My mom's cousins work here, so she visits with them while my brother and I pick apples."

"We didn't expect to see anyone we knew so far from El Monte," I said. *And away from your bully friends*, I thought. "By the way, the pup's name is Buddy."

"It's boss that you get to visit here all the time," said Pete.

"Follow me, and I'll show you something else that's boss," said Stu.

We followed Stu between the rows of apple trees and out of the orchard to a barn-type building. I looped Buddy's rope around my arm, so he wouldn't get tangled in it. Stu pointed to a big window. Pete and I pressed our faces against the glass. We watched a machine pressing apples into liquid. Buddy panted to cool off after dashing around.

"That's a 1932 cider press. It makes hundreds of gallons of

delicious apple cider every day," said Stu as he bent over to tickle Buddy's snout. "Isn't the press cool?"

"Really cool," said Pete. "I'll tell Mom to buy apple cider to take home."

"I know *lots* of cool stuff about Oak Glen," said Stu.

"Tell us the history of this place," I said. "I've never been here before."

"Okay," said Stu. "This community called Oak Glen is in a mile-high valley that's about fifteen miles east of the city of San Bernardino. Around us are the San Bernardino and the Little San Bernardino Mountains. Over there is Wilshire Peak." Stu pointed up at a craggy mountain, and Buddy's head followed the motion of his hand.

"The Cahuilla and Serrano Indians originally settled here. They harvested acorns from the oak trees in the valley. Years later, other settlers claimed land and planted potatoes. They harvested "taters" until the apple trees matured. It takes ten years for an apple tree to produce fruit."

"I didn't know that," said Pete. "I'm glad they waited patiently for the apples so all these years later I could enjoy Oak Glen apple pie. Yum."

"After lunch, we're all enjoying a piece of hot apple pie," I said. "You can join us if you want to." Buddy nodded his head up and down then sniffed at the cinnamon-scented air.

"I'll ask my mom," said Stu. "Do you want any more information?"

"What do you know about *this* place since you have family here?" I asked as I shifted my bucket of apples.

"I know this ranch was started around 1906," said Stu. "It's one of the largest ranches in Oak Glen with hundreds of acres of trees. Before World War II, the different orchard owners sent apple-filled wagons pulled by teams of horses down the canyons. Rome Beauty apples got shipped to stores all over America and around the world.

"After the war, Oak Glen ranchers like the Law family, the Parrish family, and others opened roadside stands to sell apples, apple butter, fresh-pressed cider, jams, pies, and baked goods. You can see the different stands along the road on your way out."

"Thanks for the information," said Pete. "I'm feeling wiser and hungrier for apple pie. We'll see you later or back at school on Monday. Let's go eat our meal, Buddy."

"Thanks, Stu," I said. "It was fun to see you and learn about this place."

"You're welcome," said Stu as he slung a canvas bag over his shoulder.

"Wow!" whispered Pete as we wandered away. "Stu seems different today."

"He's a nice guy," I said. "He showed us the cider press and told us about Oak Glen. He helped Mary Jane pick apples even though she was really mean to him."

As we moved to the picnic area, Pete said, "Stu surprised us, but Mary Jane's actions were no surprise. She loves to boss everyone around, and she's not very nice." Buddy growled a low *grrrr* sound as Pete glanced up.

"What are you looking for in the sky?" I asked as I looked up, too, and noticed long banks of white puffs trailing from fluffy clouds. *There's wind in the atmosphere.*

Pete said, "I'm looking for a flock of birds to dump on my sister like they did last summer." Buddy whimpered at Pete's words like he understood them and didn't want a repeat of that adventure.

"I'm not wishing for that to happen to her again," I said. "She still blames *me* for the stinky bird stuff that rained down on her. I couldn't control those birds, huh, Buddy." The big puppy wagged his tail as we left our apple-filled buckets next to Hawk's car.

Back at the picnic tables, our hungry group gathered around

the food. Hawk said a nice prayer, and we dug in. Hawk's friend, Tim, limped with his crutches to our table while Hawk carried a plate of food for him. Buddy dodged Hawk's steps while keeping his beady eyes on the loaded plate that might drop a morsel of people food.

As I watched the overgrown puppy chase Hawk, I thought about Tim. *He told us not to feel sorry for him because he had polio. So we help Tim when he needs help. He feels good that he gets around with leg braces and crutches.*

"Thanks for carrying my plate, Hawk," said Tim as he settled on a bench. He smiled and dug into the food pile on his plate. *Tim is crippled from polio, but there's nothing crippled about his appetite. Judging by the crunching and slurping sounds under the table, Buddy's appetite isn't crippled either.*

"This is great fried chicken, Mom," complimented Pete. "Thanks for putting out our picnic while we picked apples and visited with Stu."

"Who's Stu?" asked Pete's mom.

"He's that new boy that lives across the street from us back in El Monte. He showed us a cider press through that window over there." Pete pointed at the buildings.

I said, "He helped Mary Jane and Mandy pick apples from the treetops and told us lots of Oak Glen history."

"That boy lives across the street from us and goes to Cherrylee School?" asked Mary Jane. "He had overalls on, so I thought he was a really slow worker."

Pete scowled at her and said, "You could have thanked him for helping you."

"Okay, Kids, that's more than enough," said Pete's mom as she gave Mary Jane "the look" that moms give kids for being bad. "Mary Jane, let's have a talk about manners after our meal." Buddy tilted his beagle head sideways and listened.

Boy, if looks could vaporize people, then Mary Jane just vaporized us. I stared at my paper plate. As I put a spoonful of coleslaw in my mouth, Pete nudged me to look up. A flock of geese flew overhead in a V formation. Buddy followed their flight pattern while I stifled a laugh.

After our late lunch, we left Buddy with Mrs. Hawking and departed for the River Ranch bakery and indoor eating area. The chilly afternoon wind stung my face. Over by the pumpkin-filled wagon, Hawk and his friends talked to a tall, blond teenager.

Pete looked their way and said, "I think that's Stu's older brother, Barrett."

We passed the teens and entered the warm bakery. Blissful baking smells wafted around us like invisible waves. We ordered hot, plump apple pie slices smothered in vanilla ice cream. Stu waved to us from the eating area where he sat with his family.

Once we were seated at a table with our desserts, Pete whispered to me between delicious bites, "I hope Stu is nice to us when we get back to school and see him in class. I have a bad feeling that he acts a certain way with his friends and a different way when they're not around."

"I like Stu, so I'm praying that he gets out of the weather," I said.

Pete looked out the windows and said, "What weather?"

"I'm talking about the dark and stormy attitudes that Stu's friends have which encourages their bad choices," I said. "His friends are bullies. Maybe they're bullying Stu, too, like the other school kids. And . . . they're good at it, so no one catches them."

"While you're praying about weather-related-attitudes and bullies, you'd better pray about Mary Jane's stormy attitude," said Pete. "My sister, the bully, is heading this way, and her face looks like a thundercloud!"

Mary Jane hurried in our direction. Yikes. *Is it too late to hide under the table? Can I run out the side door? O God, help us, please,* I prayed.

FEROCIOUS FALL

She stopped at our table and said, "Thanks a lot, Pete, for tattling on me to Mom. You're such a cry baby. Keep your mouth shut if you know what's good for you."

After thundering her harsh words at Pete, Mary Jane turned and stomped away. Her blonde curls bounced on her back above . . . a big splat of something orange and gooey-looking. It dribbled down her pink sweater and onto her jeans.

"What's on Mary Jane's back that she doesn't know about . . . yet?" I asked Pete.

Pete took another bite of his pie and said, "I think my sister accidentally leaned back against a rotten pumpkin. Look at those pumpkin seeds mixed in with that gooey, orange stuff. At least it's not bird droppings. Rotten pumpkin must smell better . . . or not? She'll go ape when she discovers her messy attachment and the dusty stains on her front."

"At least she can't blame us for her pumpkin mess . . . or can she?" I asked.

Pete shrugged his shoulders and said, "She always blames us, so be prepared."

I swallowed my last bite of pie and said, "I read that apples are mostly eaten raw like the one you ate in the orchard. They clean your teeth and mouth. Plus, they're full of vitamins and nutrients as well as pectin which is good for digestion."

"My mom says the same thing," said Pete as he put down his fork and stood up to leave. "She also says an apple a day keeps the doctor away."

"That's a good one to remember," I said. "Let's go help your family load the apples into Hawk's Ride for the trip home."

While filling the car's trunk, Hawk and his friends talked about Stu's brother. Pete picked up Buddy, and we ducked into Hawk's Ride to listen to the teens' conversation.

Hawk said, "It's *crazy* to see Barrett here in Oak Glen. I'm used to seeing him at school or on the football field. He's Coach's golden boy."

Pete's mom and the girls scooted onto the back seat with us. A rotten, sweet smell filled the car's interior. Mary Jane wrinkled her nose and looked in my direction.

Hawk's Ride rolled out of the parking lot with a *VROOM, VROOM*. The western sky glowed in rosy, gold colors resembling Oak Glen apples. We motored by roadside stands advertising their wares on signs and with fancy labels on wood crates. Out of the radio blared a song by Bill Hayes called, "The Ballad of Davey Crockett."

Buddy nestled on my lap and looked a little like the coonskin cap worn by Davy Crockett in the TV series. I looked at Pete as I thought about our Oak Glen gathering and the sweet-smelling apples that filled the trunk. I glanced out the window and noticed swirling leaves raining down from lofty trees and littering the roadside.

I whispered to Pete, "Our moms can make pies and apple-sauce with the apples we picked. Yum. It was fun to pick apples and have autumn leaves falling around us."

Pete whispered back, "We, also, had fun talking to Stu. I wonder how he'll act at school on Monday. Will he choose to be mean like his friends?"

"I hope not," I said and petted Buddy. I leaned back as Hawk's Ride rumbled towards home. *I hope Stu makes wise choices. But will he?*

4

Dust Devil Danger

"Stu---pid, Stu---pid, Stu---pid," snarled Rex. The other kids on Cherrylee's playground kept their distance. We did, too, for a moment, until Pete turned in Stu's direction and I followed. *Rex is scary, but we have sound minds to make wise choices.*

Rex stepped back as Pete moved forward. "Hi, Guys," said Pete. "Can I help with something?"

"Hi, Pete," said Stu. His face flushed several colors of pink embarrassment. "I accidentally stepped on Rex's new shoes. That was pretty stupid and clumsy of me."

"Yeah," said Rex. "Stu does some really stupid and uncool things. He deserves to get yelled at. I don't like big, brown stains on my new shoes."

We all looked down at the brown playground dust sticking to Rex's new, denim-colored tennis shoes. When Rex stamped his feet, the dust flew off and back onto the playground. His shoes looked brand new again. *No harm done,* I thought.

"Hey, Stu, you got lucky," said Neil, the other bully in Rex's gang of three. "We won't have to beat you up for doing something *so* stu . . . pid on Columbus Day."

"Smile, Kids, 'cause a teacher's walking this way," warned Rex as a third grade teacher passed by us without stopping. "Let's cut out, Guys." Rex and Neil stomped away with Stu trail-

■ 43 ■

ing behind them like a whipped and wounded puppy dog.

"Stu stands a head taller than either of his *so-called* friends, yet he lets them hurt and humiliate him," I whispered to Pete. "I don't get it. I wish Stu could get a little courage from the story of Christopher Columbus. He didn't listen to the bullies who tried to stop his exploration to unknown places. Now we celebrate his success."

"Stu grew up with them in his old neighborhood, so he thinks he owes them," said Pete. "I wanted to pound on Rex for calling Stu names, but I don't want to get in trouble for fighting at school. I'd rather talk than fight. That's what Hawk says to do."

"I wish we could help Stu," I said as Pete and I traversed the playground where kids played Dodgeball and others lined up to play Kickball.

Heat waves rose up around the playground as sweaty students dashed from playing Foursquare to playing Tether Ball to playing Marbles on the dusty ground. Lots of little kids sat in swings and lifted off the ground. Their saddle shoes skimmed the blue sky filled with floating, piled-up cumulus clouds. *Cumulus is a Latin word for 'heap.'*

My sisters waved at me as they waited in line for the seesaw. Cloud shadows created puffy designs across the playground. *Buddy would be chasing those for sure.*

Pete motioned me towards the crowd choosing teams for Kickball. Bob Bailey called out, "Over here, Pete. Be on our team. You too, Carol Ann. You can be outfielders." Rex and his friends joined the other team.

We lined up on Bob Bailey's team. Someone had already put out the bases. "I love this game," said Pete. "It's easier to kick a big, rubbery ball with my foot than it is to hit a small baseball with a bat."

The opposing team scrambled to their places on the field. The first kicker on our team lobbed the ball to the pitcher and got tagged out when he fled to first base manned by Rex. One after another of our teammates sent the ball soaring into the outfield and raced around the bases. For the second time, Rex roughly tagged out another player.

"Watch this kick, Carol Ann," whispered Pete as he stepped to home base. He stood in front of the catcher and waited for the pitcher to roll the ball. She sent it flying across the ground with all her might. When that ball met Pete's foot, it zoomed like a rocket ship past the pitcher, past second base, and past the outfielder.

"Yea! Go Pete!" I yelled as Pete sprinted flat out around the first two bases and stopped at third. He smiled a broad grin, gave me a thumbs-up sign, and hunched over to get ready to scramble home. "I'll try to bring you in!" I called out to him. I launched the ball way out into left field. Then I scurried to first base so Pete could escape to home.

"Good kick, Carol Ann!" complimented Bob Bailey. Then he turned to the rest of the team and loudly said, "Get with it, Kids. The score is five to zero with two outs."

I waited on first base next to Rex. "That was some kind of sissy kick," snarled Rex in my ear. I inched away from him and got ready to run. "Our team will smash you guys as soon as it's our turn to be 'up.' I'll show you how to *kick* a ball."

Becky kicked the ball and bolted to first. I darted to second base as Rex reached out, caught the kickball, stepped on the base, and tagged Becky out. He chased me, slammed the ball into my back, and called out, "They're both out, and we're up."

I stumbled a few steps but kept myself from falling. Rex laughed out loud like a hyena as he ran towards home and his chance to 'show me how to kick the ball.' The rest of our team ran for their places on the field.

Pete joined me in the outfield. He said, "Are you okay, Carol Ann? Did Rex ram the kickball into your back? Becky was the third out, so he didn't need to tag you."

"He tagged me on purpose with the ball then he played it off by laughing," I said. "I'm okay. I didn't fall down or anything."

I fumbled around in my skirt pocket and pulled out my notepad. Pete watched me then said, "Did you write down another boss Bible verse?"

"I sure did," I said as I looked over to see Rex's team. They weren't ready, so I opened the notepad and read, "Psalm 18:3 says, 'I call upon the LORD, who is worthy to be praised, and I am saved from my enemies.'" I tucked the notepad back in my pocket.

"Wow, Carol Ann, that's so cool you wrote down *that* Bible verse to help you face your enemies." Pete glanced at our opponents. "What other new verses are written in your notepad?"

"More verses to help us with bullies and verses about weather so I can memorize them," I said as I heard a yell and watched our first base kid catch a fly ball.

"Out," yelled Bob. A different girl moved up to home base and kicked the ball.

Bob stopped the ball and threw it to first after she had jumped on the base. "Lucky girl!" said Pete as he looked around then over to the street. "Have you seen Hawk yet? He's supposed to drop Buddy off during our lunch recess for Show and Tell."

"I've been watching for them," I said.

Beads of sweat glistened on Pete's face as he stooped to catch a ball and threw it to the third base kid. "This is an Indian summer day," I said to Pete. "Even though it's autumn, it feels like summer with the temperatures rising up like that dust over there."

A patch of dust swirled around like a miniature whirlwind then settled back down in a poof. *What's that dust thing Mrs. Rose had talked about in science? It forms on hot days when weather conditions are just right.*

Now Rex stood at home plate. He needed a home run kick to bring his teammates in and tie our score. When the kickball bounced off his shoe, it sailed into the air and to my part of the outfield. *Yikes.* The ball flew over my head like an airplane. I turned and chased it. As it slowed down, I picked it up and flung it to our pitcher who flung it home.

"Out!" yelled a boy before Rex slid into home base.

Rex jumped up screaming, "I'm safe! That was a home run!" As he yelled, the warning bell "yelled" the end of our lunch recess. Wind waves stirred up the dirt again.

Rex dusted himself off while glaring at me. Pete went up to him and said, "Tough luck, Rex. That was a killer kick. You can get us back tomorrow."

"No thanks," he snarled. "This is a sissy game. I've got better things to do, like playing Dodgeball." He stormed off while waving for Stu and Neil to follow him. The wind pushed at their backs like it wanted to blow them off the playground.

The wind lifted up my skirt and blew my brown hair into my eyes. Pete turned to me and said, "While Bob's talking to those kids over there, we'd better gather up the equipment before the wind blows it away. Let's load this stuff into the shed while we're waiting out here for Hawk to drop Buddy off."

In the midst of our gathering process, Bob Bailey jogged up and said, "You really agitated the gravel around those bases. And Carol Ann's boss throw got Rex out."

Bob saluted, threw a few bases inside the shed, and took off for our classroom. Pete and I had special permission to wait for Buddy's arrival. While I finished putting equipment in the shed, I smiled at Bob's compliment. Before closing the door, Pete pointed to a stray dodgeball by the back fence.

We raced there to retrieve the ball. When I bent over to pick

FEROCIOUS FALL

it up, I heard a loud, earsplitting sound behind me like a giant-sized engine. I turned to see what teenager had trespassed onto the schoolyard with his hot rod. *No teen ever roared like the twister twirling towards us! Yikes!*

I heard screaming. Beyond the twisting dust, children fled fearfully across the playground. They ducked behind buildings and dodged into open classroom doors. A teacher rounded up a group of terrified first-graders. The dust roared and twisted between us and the safety of Cherrylee's buildings.

"What is it, Pete?" I screamed above the roar. "Where can we hide?"

"We're trapped on this side of that monster!" yelled Pete. "Rising air, from heat transfer that causes cumulus clouds to form, also formed that. Follow me, Carol Ann! Let's hide behind the shed over there."

I rushed after Pete through the dusty air that spun around us. Pete's hair flew up like brown waves on his head. My hair whipped in the wind as I ducked next to Pete, who ducked in front of the equipment shed. Choking dust swirled around us. We leaned against the shed and I peeked through my fingers to see this wild weather thing. Pete held out his arms like he was KID COURAGEOUS when the twister rushed toward us on the heated ground.

"Pete, is that a tornado?" I asked with a shrill voice.

"No, Carol Ann, it's a giant dust devil," said Pete. "Remember, we learned about them in class. And it's twisting our way!"

The huge, swirling dust devil roared across the vacant playground like a runaway train off its tracks. Bands of grit twirled round and round and round. Papers, rocks, dust, a dodge ball, wrappers, and trash twisted and turned in the dust devil's vortex. The dust and debris flew closer to our hiding place. *Yikes!*

Will this monstrous dust devil pick us up, too? Can we escape? O

■ 48 ■

God, help us, please, I prayed as the dust devil drew nearer and nearer. Bits of sand stung my arms. My hair blew back from my face as I gasped in fear. Somewhere close by a car door slammed, and someone yelled.

Pete nodded his head sideways for me to follow him. I turned over onto my knees and scurried behind Pete and away from the dusty whirlwind. We crawled like two babies around the shed's corner. *Is this a wise choice to find better protection? I hope so.* From our semi-safe position, we peeked around the corner and watched the dust devil.

"Get back here, Buddy," shouted a faint voice in the distance. "You're in danger!"

"Pete, did you hear that?" I asked. "I think I heard Hawk yelling for Buddy to get away from danger."

"I can't hear anything but that ferocious fury out there," shouted Pete.

I got up to peek around the shed's other corner just as Buddy bounded around it. His leash trailed behind him as he sprang into my arms. His wet tongue slopped puppy kisses on my cheek. Buddy barked then scrambled off of my lap to stand next to Pete. The pup howled and bellowed and bayed. Then he shook like a feather duster.

"Are you kids all right?" asked Hawk as he ducked down beside us. "That twister is massive! It's hovering on the other side of this shed. It could pick up this wooden box like a toy!"

"What do you want us to do?" asked Pete as he wiped dirt from his face.

"Let's scram for my car," said Hawk. "That dust can't pick up Hawk's Ride."

"No, it can't," said Pete. "But it could pick *us* up on our way there! Let's watch it. If it moves away from us, then we'll cut out for your car."

As soon as the words left Pete's mouth, the dust devil moved away from the shed, away from us, and towards the swing set with its steel poles and chains. The swirling dust twisted in and out of the swings, seesaw, and slide like a kid having fun. Then a dodgeball flew out of the dust devil as if its dusty arm flung it in a game.

Buddy barked once again and pulled at his leash like he planned to chase away the twisting menace. He stopped short when his collar held him back, because I held his leash. "You stay here until that tricky twister is gone," I told the puppy and patted his head.

"Buddy thinks he saved the day," said Pete. "I bet his doggy brain thinks he chased away the dust devil by barking at it."

"I think you're right," I said as I looked around the corner. The dust monster swirled and twirled near the slide then it changed direction. Buddy barked a woof warning. "Yikes," I said. "The twister is moving our way again!"

"Let's make ourselves scarce by running to my car," said Hawk.

"Yeah, let's get out of this dust," I coughed. "Let's go, Buddy."

We scurried like scared rats from our hiding place. The dust devil advanced behind us like a freight train. *And we're on its tracks!* We vaulted into Hawk's Ride like Olympic athletes and slammed the doors. Buddy scrambled up to look out the side window and howled with a doleful cry. *Will the dust devil follow us and lift up Hawk's Ride? Are we safe in this car?* I wondered.

The dust devil whirled across a patch of dirt in the schoolyard and puffed up even taller like a brown snake against the blue sky. Then it swung over to our previous hiding place that we had vacated only moments ago. Dangerous debris engulfed the shed. Roof tiles broke loose, and glass exploded out of the windows like deadly glass missiles.

"We moved just in time," I said with a shaky voice. "That glass would have cut us." Buddy barked in agreement as his head followed the progress of the twister.

"Mrs. Rose told us in science class to make good choices about bad weather situations, and we did," said Pete. "We hid behind the shed, and then we sprinted to the safety of this car when we had the chance. I can't wait to tell her about this during Show and Tell today. Hey, look at that."

The dust devil finished torturing the shed and twisted off past all the school buildings to the far end of the school yard. It still looked monstrous and destructive, but at least it twirled away from us and Cherrylee School. It roared through the fence and twisted up the street carrying its load of papers and debris.

"It's gone," said Pete as he exhaled his breath. "Does that dust devil remind you of anyone?"

"No," I said from the car's back seat. "Who does it remind you of?"

Hawk said, "Yeah, Pete, who does it remind you of? Don't say Mary Jane in a temper." We waited to hear his answer. Buddy sniffed as if to say, "Not me."

"The dust devil reminds me of Rex and how his hot air hurts people. Also, he's loaded down with all kinds of debris and bad stuff swirling around and spewing out at others," said Pete.

"That sounds like a match. Some kids are like that," said Hawk.

"We need to pray for Rex," I said. "He's bad news, so we need to make wise choices about dealing with him and getting out of his way like we did with the dust devil. Remember, God hasn't given us a spirit of fear, even though I was very fearful a minute ago. He gives us a spirit of power, love, and a sound mind to make wise choices."

"We made a wise choice to leave the shed for the car," said Pete.

"Time to choose to go to class," said Hawk. "See ya later."

"Thanks for bringing Buddy and giving us a safe place to hide," I said as Pete and I left the car and crossed the street to our school. Hawk fired up his hot rod. *VROOM, VROOM.* He waved from his open window when he split the scene.

Buddy pulled on his leash as he led the way. Pete said, "That dust devil went ape . . . it acted really angry, but I wasn't scared at all."

"Sure, Pete," I said. "That's why you did your KID COURAGEOUS stance."

"Well, I was a little scared of that monster twister," said Pete.

"I was too," I admitted. "Surviving a dangerous dust devil, a crazy cloudburst, a future flash flood in the San Gabriel Valley, a possible lightning strike, and the bullies who want to hurt us is turning this fall into something *ferocious.* That word means 'fierce, wild, and savage.' Kind of like how Rex feels about me since I got him out in Kickball."

"Good word, Carol Ann," said Pete as we approached our classroom. "So far we've survived a ferocious fall that's fierce, wild, and savage."

That's easy for you to say, I thought. *But can we survive the next wild weather encounter during this ferocious fall? Will we make wise choices? What about the bullies who remind us of weather?*

5

Sturtevant Falls

"Chantry Flats," yelled the little kids as Uncle Charlie drove his 1948, black Plymouth Sedan into the parking lot. He drove past the picnic tables under lofty oak trees as he circled to park. "God's Country," by Frank Sinatra, played on the car radio.

"Here we go," said my uncle as he pulled into a parking spot in front of a rock retaining wall with a pile of fireplace logs stacked on top of it. Behind the logs and up some steps sat a cabin in the shade of a monstrous tree. That same shade covered Uncle Charlie's Plymouth. Already the day felt hot as we vacated the car at ten a.m. on this Saturday morning.

"Whew," said Pete as he swiped an arm over his face. "It's gonna be a hot one today. Dad said it's a Santa Ana wind day. He said it's really blowing out in San Bernardino and Riverside this morning."

Uncle Charlie gathered his canteen and rope. As he put his Pith helmet on his head, he said, "Those Santa Ana winds are strong and dry, offshore winds that sweep across Southern California at this time of year. The humidity in the air goes way down when those devil winds blow through valleys and canyons like we're hiking in today."

"Yikes. Do we need to worry about wildfires?" I asked Uncle Charlie.

He reached out and touseled my hair as he glanced up at the treetops. "I see a faint breeze up there, so I think we're safe to hike in Big Santa Anita Canyon. The bad winds are out in the San Bernardino and Riverside areas today like Pete's dad said. We don't have to worry about the wind, but the air is heating up, so let's get going."

"Yeah, let's get going," said Pete, the Boy Scout adventurer.

I tied Buddy's long rope to his collar, threaded the other end through a belt loop on the waist of my jeans, and curled the extra rope on my arm. "Let's go, Buddy."

Across the parking lot, in front of the pack station, waited a row of horses getting loaded up for their trip into the canyon. "Let's hurry so we don't get behind those horses," said Uncle Charlie. "We'll be eating their dust, and we'll have to step around their road apples."

Pete whispered behind his hand, "What's a road apple?"

I laughed and whispered back, "That's the nasty, steaming stuff that falls from the horse's hindquarters." Pete nodded his acknowledgement and smiled. "They use horses, mules, donkeys, and even big dogs to pack stuff to the cabins in the canyon. It's the only way to get heavy supplies in there."

"Then let's split so we're not behind them," said Pete.

Our group turned at the signpost with the words "Sturtevant Falls--2 miles." We walked downhill on a broad expanse of dirt road. Dust blew up in our faces along with gnats and flies that buzzed around our heads and necks.

Dry, brown grass lined the sides of this fire road, while pine trees and mesquite leaned over and shaded our way. Trees, shrubs, and granite outcroppings covered the rolling hills all around us and in the distance.

"How far is it to the bottom of this hill?" asked Pete as he wiped his face with his hand. "It feels like we're on *The Oregon*

Trail in that old movie with John Wayne."

"That's a cool movie," I said. "This trail isn't as long as the Oregon one. It's about four hundred feet down to the canyon floor and we're almost there." I let out more rope as Buddy sniffed and explored the brush next to us along the road.

"Why is Buddy tied up?" asked Pete. "Let him chase some squirrels or rabbits."

"He would love that," I said. "I wish he could run free. But he could get lost. Or he might find a rattlesnake or a pack of hungry coyotes. Rattlesnake poison or coyotes would hurt Buddy. Last time we visited here a bunch of hikers called frantically for their lost dog."

"Hey, Buddy. I guess you're stuck on the end of that rope," said Pete to the big puppy that ran over to us with his white-tipped tail wagging furiously. Buddy barked as if to say he understood my concerns and didn't like snakes either.

At the bottom of the road, we traveled past another sign with the words: "Gabriolino Trail." The sign also pointed the way to "Sturtevant Falls--1 1/4 miles." Oak, alder, bay, and spruce trees surrounded us. Our group moved into much-needed shade under a fall-colored, leafy canopy.

Uncle Charlie pointed to a bridge crossing a flowing creek and said, "That way."

The little kids crossed the wooden footbridge into Robert's Camp. Ahead of us, Buddy sniffed as he scampered over the bridge and pulled me behind him. Pine scent wafted to my nose. Various noises surrounded us. *Yha, yha, yha,* chattered hidden squirrels. *Che, che, che,* chirped busy birds as bugs buzzed overhead in the warm air.

On the other side of the green-painted bridge, we veered to the right. "The Gabriolino Trail sign reminds me of the dream I had last summer when we visited the Los Angeles Arboretum," I said.

"Yeah, I remember," said Pete. "The visit to the Arboretum was a blast."

"It sure was," I said as I looked at the rustling bushes only a few feet away.

An old cabin nestled in the woods above us on a boulder-strewn slope. A rock fireplace clung to the cabin's wooden wall. Giant trees leaned in around it. Dead leaves covered the ground up to an outhouse in the forest. Birds twittered in the trees.

"Who owns that old place?" asked Pete.

"I don't know who owns it," I answered as we stepped along the narrow trail. "These are vacation cabins built in the early 1900s during the "Great Hiking Era" of 1895 to 1938. During that time, people built cabins here on the trail that Wilbur Sturtevant carved through the canyon. The falls we're going to see are named after him."

"Old Wilbur Sturtevant did a good job on this trail," observed Pete as he shuffled in the dust.

"It's our favorite hiking trail," I said. "I can't believe you've never hiked it with us."

We passed more cabins and a sign with the words: "Fern Lodge Junction." We stepped along the rocky path through what looked like a jungle of trees, shrubs, blackberry bushes, and more trees. Our feet made a *crunch, swish* sound as we pushed through the fallen leaves that littered the walkway. The trees slowly swayed in the welcome breeze.

"Does anyone ever rob these cabins?" asked Pete as we passed more of them.

"I don't think they have much of value in them to rob," I said. "And the crooks would have an uphill hike out of here carrying their loot."

"Hey, Carol Ann," said Pete as we kept hiking. "Are you still writing down notes about burglaries? Do you think they're connected to Rex and his friends? My dad read about three burglaries in Tuesday's newspaper. Did you write notes about those articles?"

"I did, because I heard Mom talking to Dad about the crime in El Monte. I don't know if they're connected to Rex," I said as we crunched leaves under our shoes. Buddy had all the rope now and foraged through bristly bushes.

"Rex is our age, so it's hard to believe he could be a burglar," said Pete. "But I guess a criminal can start their career at any age."

"I'm writing down anything I read, see, or hear about in the notepad that I keep in my pocket." I patted my jeans pocket with my right hand.

"I hate to mention it, but Dad's giving blood since he read the article about the Bloodmobile being in town next Tuesday," said Pete. "Are you gonna give blood?"

"I heard about that, too," I said. "I asked Uncle Charlie about it, and he said we're too young to give blood." I smiled in relief and glanced up the trail at Uncle Charlie who led the way.

"Doctor Charles would know," said Pete. "Did you see the story about the Cub Scout Powwow and the Big Cheese at Crawford's Market?" Buddy ran back in our direction at the mention of cheese. His tongue dangled out of his mouth like an extra ear while he panted for air.

"Are you thirsty, Buddy?" I asked my big puppy as I led him to the creek. Water flowed around groups of boulders. Buddy scurried into the stream and lapped at it. Pete bent down to the water above where Buddy lapped and cupped cold water up to his mouth.

I did the same then said, "Mom didn't mention the Powwow story but she told me about Crawford's Market having the Big Cheese."

Pete finished slurping water like a puppy and said, "My mom says we're gonna go see it next Thursday. They're giving away dinners with baked beans, creamy coleslaw, potato rolls, and chunks of the Big Cheese." He licked his lips in anticipation.

Once again Buddy lifted his head up and looked in Pete's direction at the mention of food. I dug doggy treats out of my pocket and gave him some. Buddy barked out a doggy thank-you. Then he explored the nearby bushes and boulders as we hurried to catch up with Uncle Charlie and the youngsters who chattered like chipmunks.

I said, "Crawford's Market is so cool to have the Big Cheese every year for its Fall Festival. I'm gonna ask Mom and Dad to take us there for dinner, so Mom gets a break from cooking."

The treetops rippled like waves at the beach. Pete looked up at the waving trees and said, "This place reminds me of the movie called, *The Adventures of Robin Hood*, with Errol Flynn. Robin Hood's merry men hid out in a forest just like this one."

"I loved the costumes that Maid Marion wore in that old movie," I said. "Olivia DeHaviland played the part of Maid Marion. She was so pretty and brave." A dark part of the forest loomed up ahead. "Hurry up, Pete, this is the scariest place in the canyon, and I like to blast through it." Buddy pulled on the rope as if he was in a hurry, too.

We quickly sprinted through the creepy part of the forest. I gulped in courage like taking a drink of life-saving water. Great, gnarled arms of giant, dark trees hung over the trail. A hollowed-out tree made this a scary, creepy, horrible Halloween forest and not a friendly forest at all. *Yikes.*

At Fiddler's Crossing, we passed another cabin then crossed the creek. Buddy splashed through the cascading creek water. I balanced on one slippery rock after another. Pete and Buddy scampered to the shady bank and watched me while they waited.

"Do you need some help, Carol Ann?" Pete laughed while Buddy barked.

"I'm right behind you," I said as I hopped onto dry ground. "I didn't want to get my tennis shoes wet and feel that yucky, slippery feeling inside of them." *Crackle, crackle* sounded from a nearby bush. I jumped.

"Let's investigate," said Pete. "I'd like to see a Pacific rattlesnake. We missed seeing one last July when we visited Lytle Creek Canyon."

Buddy barked a sharp, explosive cry at the rattling brush.

"Stay by me, Buddy," I said. "Yikes. This is no time to meet a rattlesnake." I curled his rope around my arm and started up the trail once again. I peered at the vegetation surrounding us. *Rex calls me a worrywart, and I am. I need to trust God to protect me, because I do worry about seeing snakes on this hike.*

"I bet Maid Marion wasn't afraid of snakes," said Pete as we headed into an area of the hike that really did look like a jungle. Ferns and strange, claw-like plants enclosed the trail and left little room for getting by them. Spiky leaves scratched at my jeans and bare arms. I leaped like a dancer as a stick flew up from Pete's shoe.

Uncle Charlie and the kids disappeared around a corner of giant, ten-foot-high, granite boulders. Trees and shrubs still sprinkled the rocky trail with shadows. Excited voices echoed in the distance. *Did Uncle Charlie and the kids make it to the falls? Or did they find a big, fat rattlesnake sunning itself on a boulder?*

Pete and Buddy rushed around the ten-foot granite sentinels that flanked the trail and disappeared. I stumbled along behind them, scrambling over a pathway of rocks that looked like they had been tossed there by a giant. I hiked into a clearing and stared . . . at Sturtevant Falls.

The falls dribbled fifty feet down a craggy rock wall, over a rocky outcropping, and then tumbled watery fingers into a rock-lined, natural pool. Leaves floated across the pool's surface like small copper boats racing to shore. Cascading water danced into the pool and sent ripples across the water in ever-expanding circles.

The kids played on the edge of the pool while the waterfall splashed behind them. Buddy yanked at his rope to break free of restraint. I loosened all the rope he needed so he could splash into the water for a drink.

Pete stood still as he looked up, down, and all around. He said, "This is fat city. What a great place!" Pete turned in a circle and glanced around some more. "It's like a paradise, Carol Ann. I wonder if this is how the Garden of Eden looked."

Rock walls surrounded the glen on three sides. A blue sky, dotted with curly cirrus clouds, peeked above the granite walls. Enormous oak and alder trees spread their branches above and around us. Cool air brushed our faces along with splashes of spray from the falls.

"I don't know if it looks like the garden in the Bible, but it's like an Eden to the hikers who visit here . . . minus the snake, of course," I said. "God created the heavens and the earth, so why wouldn't he create a lovely place like this?"

Buddy stepped around the little kids zigzagging in and out of the shallow water on the pool's shore. Every other step he lapped at the refreshing liquid. Uncle Charlie rested on a flat rock with his pith helmet sitting next to him. His flattened, brown hair swirled against his head like a cap. He pushed at his glasses and waved me over to him.

"That was a fabulous hike to get here, wasn't it, Carol Ann?" asked my uncle. "And now we can rest in this fabulous place."

"I love it here, Uncle Charlie," I said as I sat down to rest. "This is my favorite place on the whole earth. It's so beautiful and peaceful. Thanks for finding this place and for bringing us here all the time." Buddy sniffed with a snuffling sound along the ground.

"What do you smell, little Buddy?" asked Uncle Charlie with a smile as he swatted at pesky flies. "Do you smell a little woodland creature?"

"He's telling you that this place is fabulous," I said. "And yes, he smells a woodland creature that he wants to chase." While we watched Buddy snoop around, three domesticated woodland creatures rushed into the glen then dashed up to Buddy. The three very friendly, white German shepherds introduced themselves to my pup.

Their owner trailed behind them with a fistful of leashes in his hand. "They're friendly," he called. "They won't hurt anyone. I didn't know you were here, or I would have kept them on their leashes. I'm really sorry."

Uncle Charlie said, "That's no problem. Your dogs look mighty friendly."

Buddy and the shepherds splashed around in the water at the pool's edge then sniffed among the wet rocks and at each other. The little kids hid behind Uncle Charlie who introduced himself to our visitor as Dr. Charles McCammon.

"Nice to meet you, Dr. Charles," said our visitor, named Steve, as he shook Uncle Charlie's hand. "I'll round up my dogs so the kids won't be afraid." Steve called Brandy, Cherry, and Snoops over to him then clipped a leash to each one. He looked down at Buddy and said, "Nice to meet you, little guy. Enjoy the falls, everyone." Steve waved goodbye with one hand while he held his dogs with the other.

Buddy's head drooped to one side as he watched his new friends walk away. He seemed to shrug then he sniffed at more rocks in a grassy area where the creek ran out of the pool. The silver stream slipped over dark and mossy rocks as it escaped down a boulder-strewn creek bed.

A welcome breeze blew through the glen and chased away the

bugs. Uncle Charlie put his pith helmet back on his head and scooted off his rocky bench. He beckoned us to follow him back to the world outside of Big Santa Anita Canyon and Sturtevant Falls. The little kids scrambled after my uncle.

At the entrance to the glen, I glanced back, waved to the falls, and said, "See you next time." An extra-large splash seemed to say goodbye. I turned my eyes back to the trail and the boulders that needed crossing.

"Hey, Carol Ann," said Pete. "Today was a great day. Thanks for inviting me."

"You're welcome," I said as Buddy sailed over the boulders in front of us like a ship on the sea. "I'm glad you had fun and that we got away from Rex for the day."

Pete said, "Rex is like a rattlesnake that you don't want to meet on the trail."

I looked around to make sure no sneaky snake lay in wait for me. The trail looked clear of creatures. I followed Pete and my family's footprints out of the forest. *Back at school, will Pete be there to help me if Rex sends his snake venom my way?*

6

Luke's Lion Farm

"Let's create a lion farm with these giant boxes that my dad dropped off from his shop," said Pete as we stared at several stacks of boxes leaning next to his garage.

"That sounds like a fun after-school project on a smoggy day," I said as I picked up a square, three-foot by three-foot cardboard box. I held it so it wouldn't block my view.

"Let's go get the little kids, so they can help us carry these to your yard," said Pete in a muffled voice from behind a big box.

I moved behind Pete up his driveway and through the gate into our yard's play area. Buddy bolted ahead of us barking like a messenger to warn the kids. We dumped our boxes near the monkey bars where the little kids scampered around like . . . monkeys.

Little Charlie hung upside down with his blond hair hanging earthward. His upside-down mouth asked, "What are the boxes for? Can I have one?" He promptly pulled himself up and dropped down onto the soft earth below.

My two sisters, Cousin Cathie, and Mandy gathered around us and peered inside the empty boxes. "There's nuffin inside this box," said Gail with a frowning face.

"If you help us carry more boxes over here we can build a lion farm," I told the kids. "Remember when Pete told you about that lion farm that used to be in our town? Well, he can tell you the

■ 63 ■

story again then we'll build our own lion farm with boxes."

"Can we name it Luke's Lion Farm?" asked Little Charlie. "My friend Luke had his appen . . . denix out and he's at home feeling really sad. It will make him happy if we name our farm after him."

"Okay, Kid," said Pete with a smile. "We'll let you name our lion farm as long as I get to be the main lion tamer. We'll call it Luke's Lion Farm after your friend. We can make him a special lion cage with his name on it."

We hauled more than a dozen boxes of assorted sizes into our yard. "Pete, where are your postcards of how the real lion farm used to look?" I asked him as he placed the biggest box over by the sidewalk.

"I'll go home and get them while you each pick a box to be your lion cage," Pete said then sprinted home. Each kid picked a box while we waited for our lion tamer's return. Our slide and monkey bars made a boss backdrop.

In a few minutes, Pete passed back through our shared gate with several postcards in his hand. "Guess what? I saw Stu and he asked why we're hauling boxes over here. I told him about building Luke's Lion Farm. He's getting his Gay's Lion Farm postcard collection that his granddad gave him. And he's bringing over some stuffed fabric lions."

"Hey, kids, go gather up all your toy lions for the farm," I said.

Pete and the kids took off in several directions hunting for lion treasures. Buddy sniffed for doggy treasures. I spread a blanket on the grass while the kids raided their toy boxes. Soon, gold-colored, stuffed lions, wooden lions, plastic lions plus lion coloring books, and a molded, metal lion piled together in a lion heap like a mountain.

Stu slipped through our gate and deposited more stuffed lions on the pile. He said, "I've got my granddad's postcard collection. They're wrapped in plastic, so you can't hurt them. Sit down, everyone. I'll pass around the postcards and tell you what I know about that old tourist attraction."

The kids and I plunked down on the blanket. The air felt chilly, so I buttoned up my sweater and pulled down my school skirt. I looked up at the grayish, overcast sky. *Is that smog or rain clouds covering the valley? My eyes are burning, so it's smog. Yikes.*

Pete and Stu took turns telling us about the lion farm that had closed years ago. Stu passed out postcards while he told us, "Gay's Lion Farm opened up in 1925 here in El Monte. Mr. and Mrs. Gay bought five acres of land at Peck Road and Valley Boulevard for their lion farm. They were circus performers who trained lions as animal actors for the movie industry."

"I never seed a lion farm," said seven-year-old Little Charlie. "I wanna go there."

"Me too," said Gail. "I wanna tempt the lions."

"I think you mean you want to train the lions," I told Gail and stifled a laugh. "The farm is not there anymore, so you can't tempt or train lions except here in our yard."

"That's right," said Pete. "Gay's Lion Farm entertained thousands of guests over the years. In 1925, El Monte High School chose the lion as their mascot, and Mr. Gay brought a real lion to their football games. The farm was a really popular place in Southern California until it closed down in 1942. That was before any of us were born."

"Aw shucks," said Little Charlie. "I wanted to see those real lions."

Stu said, "You can see lions at the Los Angeles County Zoo. When the lion farm closed down, the lions went to different zoos. Mr. Gay's most famous lions were Slats and Jackie. They took turns roaring as the MGM trademark lion."

The kids took turns looking at the postcards then we took turns getting our boxes. We used crayons to draw bars on our "cages." Stu carefully cut out the "bars", so our lions could sit inside and look out.

After studying the postcards, we made the biggest box the main entrance with a cut-out doorway. Then we arranged the "cages" in a U with an exhibition area in the middle for the lion tamer.

Pete waved his arm and said, "Hey Kids, put that small box here in the middle. That's where the lion can sit when he gets trained." Pete set a good-sized, fabric lion on the box and pretended to crack a whip over its head.

"I'm gonna look in our costume box for a whip," said Kathleen as she trotted past the chicken car and over to Aunt Ruthie's back door.

"Let's get our Peter Pan dress-ups for the lion farm," said Gail.

"I'll get my grandmother's opera cape," said Cathie as she followed Gail.

Kathleen returned with a bundle of stuff that she dropped down next to the lion pile. A nice piece of yellow, four-inch-wide fringe peeked out.

"Here, Buddy," I called him over to me. "Good boy, Buddy. Let me tie this fringe around your neck so you can have a lion mane." I looped the fringe several times very loosely around Buddy's neck. When I let him go, he shook his head, danced around in a circle, then pranced off like a miniature king of beasts.

Pete picked up Buddy, tickled his white tummy, and said, "Hey there, Buddy, you look good enough to perform in the Boy Scout Parade this Saturday." He set Buddy down on top of the box in the center ring. "You can be our living lion."

The little kids put their lion food mud cookies on the slide, tucked their toy lions into their cages with muddy hands, and then climbed in with them. Their funny lion faces stared out through the bars. "Roar, roar," roared the kids from their cardboard cages.

Stu opened both ends of the leftover boxes and pushed them

together into a tunnel. "Hey, lions, when you get tired of being caged up, you can roam through this tunnel," said Stu.

"You got a Bible verse for today in your notepad?" Pete asked me.

"I do," I answered as I took my notepad from my pocket and thumbed through it. "When I was looking up weather verses, I found one that talked about a whirlwind and about lions." I read, ' . . . and their wheels like a whirlwind. Their roaring shall be like a lion, they shall roar like young lions.' Those verses are from the end of Isaiah."

"That's cool, Carol Ann," said Pete. "You find good Bible verses."

"What's cool about reading Bible verses?" mocked Mary Jane as she slithered into our yard followed by Rex and Neil. "Anyone can read a verse that's written down."

"I could read one, too," said Rex, "but I don't want to. Those verses are for goofs and worrywarts who are stu . . . pid." Rex glanced from me to Stu who still entertained the little lions in Luke's Lion Farm. *I hope Stu didn't hear Rex.*

"Carol Ann writes Bible verses down, so she can memorize them," said Pete in my defense. "She finds verses about weather and other stuff like the one she just read."

Rex strutted over to me. "What else you got in your little, red notepad? Let me see it," he said as he grabbed for my notepad which I quickly hid behind my back.

"None of your business," I said nicely. "I like to write down verses and notes about things I see like the smoggy, gray sky today or the rain we had last week."

VROOM, VROOM, roared Hawk's Ride as it rolled up Pete's driveway followed by a police car. Rex looked over at the police car, then at Neil, and said, "Let's split. The Heat's here." They cut out like two rockets.

"What's their problem?" asked Mary Jane. "And who's making all that awful noise over there?" She strolled over to investigate the lion farm. *With her blonde hair she can be queen of the lions,* I thought then shook my head no.

"Did you write that down?" asked Pete. "Did you write down that Rex floored it like a race car when he saw my dad's policeman friend pull up in the driveway? He acted like the police are looking for *him.*"

"Maybe they are," I said. "They just don't know it yet. This morning's paper had an article about three youths who strong-armed an El Monte High student."

"I saw that story, too," said Pete. "Ever since you started looking for clues in the paper, you have me reading it. I never read the paper before except for current events."

"One story talked about a burglar who used a screwdriver to pry open the lock on the door to the ice cream store. Then he ransacked the place. Luckily, he got caught."

"How can we catch a thief?" asked Pete.

"By seeing the movie, *To Catch a Thief,* with Cary Grant," I laughed. "It's playing at the El Monte Drive-in." I opened my notepad, pulled the pencil stub out of my pocket, and jotted down notes about Rex's reaction to the police car.

"Dealing with Rex gave us a break from the lions over there," said Pete. "Did I tell you I found out that Mr. Gay trained the lions that got used in the Tarzan movies? They kept them at the Los Angeles Arboretum during filming. Cool, huh?"

"That is cool," I said as we wandered back to the lion farm. The "lions" scrambled through their tunnel of boxes. Buddy waited at the tunnel entrance and licked each lion as he or she emerged.

"Yucky, Buddy," said Gail. "I got slobbered all over."

"I did, too," complained Cathie as she crawled out dragging her opera cape.

"Stu's got a pocketful of doggy treats. I gave them to him to convince Buddy the Lion to do tricks for the crowd." I laughed and settled down on the blanket to watch the show. The lions crawled inside their cages by lifting open the side flaps.

Mary Jane helped Mandy into her cage and folded the flap down. Mandy stuck her stuffed lion's face partly through the cardboard bars and roared a squeaky, baby roar. Mary Jane sat down on the end of our slide. *Yikes. Aren't the kids' lion cookies sitting there?*

Gail pawed at her bars like a real lion then called over to me, "Carol Ann, you can be a visit . . . turer. You have to clap weally loud."

"Clap really loud, Carol Ann," called Mary Jane over to me. "That is if you're not too busy writing dumb stuff down in your notepad." She shrugged her shoulders, tugged at her pink cardigan, and turned toward the show that was about to start.

Stu had a water pistol in his belt. He wore one of Uncle Charlie's old pith helmets. Stu circled the center area like Mr. Gay did in the picture postcards. Buddy bounced up and down on the box as Stu whipped a stick and string "whip."

"Now, Buddy," said Stu, "sit for the spectators and your lion friends."

Buddy obeyed and sat down. Stu leaned over to give him a treat. Then Stu picked up a hoop. "Jump, Buddy." Buddy popped up and jumped through the hoop.

Everyone clapped for the lion tamer and his tame lion named Buddy the Beagle Hound. The kids left their cages and crawled around Stu. "Roar, roar, roar," they roared like miniature motors. Stu whipped the string.

"Is that it?" complained Mary Jane as she marched in our direction. "That's the show? I sat out here in the smog, with my eyes burning, in my good school clothes for that?"

Gail stood up and said, "It's okay, Mary Jane. You can crawl frough our tunnel or play with the toy lion cwubs if you want to." Gail smiled and roared some more.

FEROCIOUS FALL

"Don't flip out, Sis," said Pete. "Join the lion tribe, and you can jump through a hoop. You might get messed up, though, when you crawl on the ground."

"You Kiddos can have your jungle, or farm, or whatever it is," she complained some more. "I'm leaving!" Mary Jane whirled around like a dust devil and stomped away towards home and a clean place to sit that wouldn't leave mud on the back of her pink, plaid skirt. *Oops.*

"Is that what I think it is on the back of my sister's skirt?" asked Pete.

"It's a mud cookie, and she'll be frosted when she sees it," I said and smiled.

"Is it our fault that she gets goopy whenever she's near us?" he asked with a shrug.

"Does anyone want a snack?" called Mom as she approached us balancing a tray of real cookies. "I made Golden Lion Cookies for you."

Mom set the tray of oatmeal cookies down in center ring. Cookies became the new stars of the show. The lion kids grabbed cookies in their lion paws and roared. "Roar, roar, roar." Pete picked up a couple of cookies, too. I waited for him to roar as well. Stu gave Buddy a treat, and my puppy roared a happy hound dog yipping noise.

Will Mary Jane roar at us when she discovers the mud mess on her skirt? Is Rex gone for the afternoon or will he be back to cause trouble?

■ 70 ■

Ferocious Football

"The Lions will *pound* the Rosemead Panthers tonight at the football game," said Pete as we rode to the game on the backseat of Uncle Charlie's 1948 Plymouth.

Gail said in a trembling voice, "I don't wanna go to the football game. I'm scare . . . ed of the lions and panther . . . ers. They will gobble us!"

From up in the front seat, Little Charlie said, "They aren't real animals, Silly. Those are the team names. Don't be such a 'fraidy cat.'"

"Let's not call each other names," said my uncle as he steered his car around a corner. "Gail's never been to a football game. That's an understandable mistake to think the team names are real animals. In fact, years ago before World War II, the owner of Gay's Lion Farm brought a *real* lion to the football games. That lion became their mascot."

Pete said, "My dad said Mr. Gay paraded the lion around the field before the game and during half time. The crowd loved seeing a real lion at the games. A Leo the Lion statue sits in front of El Monte High School as a tribute to their lion mascot."

"Didn't Hawk and his friends help The Key Club paint Leo so he would look shiny again?" I asked Pete.

"Tim, Ernie, and Hawk helped paint the lion statue because it's sitting in front of the school, and Hawk said he thought it

■ 71 ■

needed to look hip," said Pete.

"That was nice of Hawk and his friends to help out. I hope Hawk gets a touchdown in tonight's game," I said. "I don't understand many plays, but I know the football player gets points for his team when he runs into the end of the field."

"That's called the end zone," said Pete. "The lucky player that runs into the end zone with the ball, or catches a ball there, gets six points for his team."

"I hope Hawk gets touched down, too," said Gail with a big smile.

The song, "Autumn Leaves," by Nat King Cole played on the car radio. His smoky sounding voice sang, "The falling leaves drift by my window. The falling leaves of red and gold." Many falling leaves really did drift by the car's windows as we drove along.

Up ahead, bright white lights on tall, metal poles illuminated District Field for the El Monte High School versus Rosemead High School football game. Uncle Charlie drove his car into the parking lot. He parked next to a car driven to the field by one of the five thousand fans expected for the rivalry game tonight.

"Wow," said Pete. "This parking lot is hopping with cool cars. Look at that cherry machine over there. Thanks for inviting me to ride along, Dr. Charles. Hawk's team should have it made in the shade . . . a sure win."

"Let's hope so," answered Uncle Charlie. "Grab your jackets, Kids, and stay by me so no one gets lost." We scooted out of my uncle's car into the chilly night.

As Pete and I followed Uncle Charlie through the parking lot, I looked around for a black Chevy pickup truck that parked on our street all the time and the teenager who drove it. We left the parking lot and passed through the crowd to the visitor's bleachers on the south side of the football field.

Pete leaned over and whispered, "What were you looking for back there?"

Ferocious Football

"I was looking for that suspicious Chevy pickup truck we keep seeing on our street and all over town," I answered in a whisper. "I want to write down its license plate number."

"Let's go back out there and snoop around during the half time program," said Pete. "Four eyes are better than two. I've got a small flashlight in my pocket."

"I figured you had your flashlight with you," I said.

Uncle Charlie looked in my direction and asked, "Since we're so early and kickoff isn't until eight o'clock, do you and Pete want to get some snacks?"

"We'd love to go buy snacks, Dr. Charles," said Pete.

My uncle handed us money, and off we went to the snack bar located beneath the giant concrete bleachers on the other side of the field. Because Rosemead High hosted the game tonight, their fans sat in the good stands while we sat on the visiting team's portable bleachers.

We navigated through the football fans. A cool autumn breeze ruffled my hair. After waiting in line at the snack bar, we paid for and received our order. I tucked two hot dogs into my coat pocket. Then I cradled four sodas in my arms for the trip back around the field. Pete juggled the other sodas and the popcorn.

When someone bumped me, the sodas flew like miniature airplanes. I looked behind me into Rex's smiling face. He said, "Oh, sorry, Carol Ann. Did I bump you? Oh, gee, there go your sodas. Too bad."

"I'll get 'um," said Stu. "I'm sure Rex didn't mean to bump into you, Carol Ann."

Pete moved close to Rex and said, "I'm *sure* it was an accident."

Rex smirked and said, "Nice to see you guys. Hope you don't have any more *accidents* tonight." He nodded to Neil and said, "Let's leave these ankle-biters."

Stu handed me the sodas and said, "Here, Carol Ann. I gotta

go get a seat to watch the kickoff. Barrett's in the starting lineup, and a lot of scouts are watching him tonight. He's hoping for a great game and a football scholarship to a good college. See ya."

Stu disappeared into the crowd heading in our same direction. "Stu's a good guy," I said, as I wiggled the sodas back into place. "Why can't he see that Rex is bad news?"

"Stu's a loyal friend," said Pete. "He can't see how bad Rex is."

"I'm going to tell Stu the Bible story of David and Goliath," I said. "Stu's like David, and with God's help he can fight the giant bully in his life."

We tramped up into the stands and sat down next to Uncle Charlie and the kids. Pete's mom and dad waved to us from several rows over. Mary Jane glared at us then wrinkled her nose like she smelled a skunk.

"Hi, Mom and Dad," said Pete as he waved to his family.

Suddenly, the crowd around us surged to their feet like a tidal wave and screamed, "Go, Lions!"

The El Monte High School football team players raced across the field. I looked over at Gail and watched her snuggle next to Uncle Charlie. He patted her shoulder reassuringly so the Lions wouldn't *get her.*

"Go, Lions! Go, Hawk! Go, Barrett!" yelled Pete as our team, dressed in blue and white uniforms, lined up across from the Rosemead High School Panthers. Pete handed the popcorn to the kids, and we passed out the sodas. The warm hot dogs and change went from my hands to Uncle Charlie's.

My uncle glanced at his watch and said, "Looks like it'll be an eight o'clock kickoff just like the newspaper said. The paper also said this is supposed to be the finest game of the year between these two local schools. Last year the Lions beat Rosemead nineteen to six. I hope the Lions win tonight."

"I'm sure they can with no sweat," said Pete. "Look at 'em go!"

Ferocious Football

We sat down to watch 'em go. The Lion's varsity squad kicked the ball to the Panthers who fumbled the ball after two plays. As the pom-pom girls cheered our team on, the Lions moved flat out down the field against the Panthers. John "Hawk" Hawking scored the opening touchdown. The El Monte crowd stood and roared like lions.

Pete said in an excited voice, "Did you see that, Carol Ann? Hawk caught that fifteen-yard pass and floored it for a touchdown! Yea! Hawk! Way to go, Big Brother!"

"Wow!" I said. "Hawk scored the first six points of the game."

"Yeah, he sure did and look!" Pete pointed at the kicker as he kicked the football between the goalposts for one more point. "Now the score is El Monte . . . seven, and Rosemead . . . zero." Pete grinned like the crescent moon up in the night sky.

"Congratulations," said Uncle Charlie to Pete. "Only five minutes into the game and your brother has already scored a fabulous touchdown."

"Thanks, Dr. Charles," said Pete. "I'll let Hawk know how much you appreciate his souped-up performance. That's what Hawk does to a car to make it go fast."

"Thanks for the definition, Son," said Uncle Charlie with a wink.

"Anytime, Dr. Charles," said Pete. "Hey, Carol Ann, look at those paper shakers. They're really getting with it. They're doing a boss job of encouraging our team."

"They're so cute," I said, as I watched the cheerleaders shake their pom-poms while performing a routine to inspire the crowd.

"Can I be a pom-pommer girl when I grow up?" asked Gail.

"You can try out to be one when you get to high school," said Kathleen. "And they're called pom-pom girls or cheerleaders."

The two teams battled back and forth like warriors in a war. During the second period, the quarterback sent a thirty-yard pass to Stu's brother, Barrett, who ran the ball into the end zone for the second touchdown of the game. Again, the kick made it through the goal posts for the extra point. Around us, the crowd clapped and cheered like an erupting volcano.

"Now the Lions have a fourteen to zero lead over Rosemead," said Pete as he looked around. "Everyone's going ape . . . 'cause they're so excited."

Right before half time, Barrett caught another really long pass and rushed for the third touchdown of the game. The ball sailed easily between the goal posts for the extra point: Visitor . . . twenty-one . . . Home . . . zero. Again the crowd around us erupted with approval.

"Carol Ann, ask your uncle if we can say "hi" to my folks and get more snacks during half-time," said Pete.

I turned to Uncle Charlie. "Can I go with Pete?" I asked.

"Sure thing," said my uncle as he handed me money for candy. Pete and I stepped around people and scrambled over metal benches to his folks.

Mary Jane, dressed in her pink wool coat, glared at us and said, "What do you two want?" Her perfect, blonde curls wiggled as she shook her head at us. "Why are you wandering around in the stands? Sit down and watch Rosemead's Homecoming Parade."

Mandy pointed at the field and said excitedly, "Look at the queen."

And we did. Convertible cars circled the football field carrying the Homecoming Queen and Princesses. Their crowns and dresses sparkled like diamonds under the field lights. The Rosemead High School Band marched across the field playing rousing music for the Homecoming show.

"We're on our way to the snack bar," said Pete. "Does anyone want anything?"

Pete's family shook their heads no, so we took off. As we wove our way through the crowd, the announcer gave the names of the queen and her court. Pete stopped to look at the cars on the field. I looked at the queen.

"Those flip-tops . . . convertible cars . . . are really cool," said Pete in admiration. "That one looks like Ernie's '32 that we call Wild Panther. Listen to it roar."

"Flip-top is a funny name for a convertible," I said as I followed Pete into the parking lot. The announcer's voice faded into the distance.

"That was a flood of folks we had to pass through," whispered Pete as he looked around.

"Speaking about floods, Mom read in the newspaper about a terrible flood in India," I said. Pete nodded yes, so I said, "It's the worst flood disaster there in a century. I'm going to share that story for my current event at school next week."

Pete said, "My mom read about a safe that was stolen then slid out of the crook's vehicle. It was recovered, but there were two more burglaries; one at El Monte Plating Works, where steel hooks are missing, and the other article was about stuff taken from a principal's car."

"Mom shared those stories, too," I said. "If that Arroyo High principal saw us right now he'd think *we* were thieves." I stopped and pointed. "Let's go up and down these rows. And before we go back to the game, let's get my coin purse out of Uncle Charlie's car so someone doesn't steal *it*."

"Okay," said Pete. "I'll shine my flashlight at the back of those cars. Should we look for scrape marks like a safe would make if it slid out of a vehicle? Are we looking for that Chevy pickup, too?"

"Yes," I said. "That truck is the most suspicious vehicle in town. I think the driver is a teenager, so he should be here at the game tonight."

Pete waved his flashlight at car trunks and tailgates as we snuck up and down the aisles. We ducked down several times to avoid being seen by moving cars. Tall trees waved in the breeze and dropped their leaves on us like sifted flour.

"This is like the treasure hunt they're having at the El Monte Plunge tomorrow, except we're not diving into the water for coins," said Pete.

"No, we're not. This is a treasure hunt for clues," I said then stopped to listen and look. "Did you hear that?"

"Hear what?" asked Pete in a whisper. "What did it sound like?"

"It sounded like footsteps following us," I answered as I ducked down behind a Chevy station wagon. Pete dropped down next to me. My heart pounded in my ears.

The cars around us in the dark parking lot looked like huge, hulking monsters ready to spring out and attack us. Footsteps crunched upon the gravel as people approached our hiding place . . . and passed by. A couple got into a car just down from us.

I looked at Pete and wiped my forehead. "Yikes. That scared me."

"Yeah, me too," admitted Pete. "For a minute I thought someone was after us. I wasn't sure which way to run."

"Look over there, Pete," I said and pointed at the back of a black Chevy pickup illuminated in the headlights of the couple's car. "That's the truck we're searching for! Let's go!" I jumped up and bumped into a dark shape. *Yikes!*

The dark, scary shape spoke to me, "What're you doing out here in the parking lot, Carol Ann?" asked Rex as Neil snickered.

"We're just searching . . . for my uncle's car," I said. "I need to get my coin purse out of it so it doesn't get stolen."

"Yeah, we're looking for her uncle's tank and Carol Ann's coin purse," said Pete.

"Are you sure you aren't stealing from these cars?" asked Rex. "There's been a lot of that in the paper lately. I bet the police would like to know who's sneaking around in the parking lot during football games."

"I bet they would," said Pete. "I better tell them about you and Neil. What are you doing out here, anyway?"

"That's none of your business," snarled Rex. "Let's split, Neil."

As they scurried away like two guilty rats we turned our attention to the black pickup. Before we could rush down the aisle, the pickup's tail lights lit up, it reversed out of the parking space, and took off with a rumble. We hurried to where it had been parked only moments ago and stared at an empty space.

Pete pointed his flashlight at the ground and said, "What's that over there?" We followed the lighted path to a shiny sliver of a thing.

I bent over, picked up a metal hook, and held it for Pete to see it. "I think this hook may be a clue. I'll save it with the other clues," I said as I slipped it into my pocket.

■　　■　　■

Back in our seats, we watched Rosemead High score their only touchdown and extra point. At the end of the ferocious football game, a mighty cheer rose up from our bleachers. The pom-pom girls did cartwheels across the field while the football players shouted out their victory.

As we left the stands, Uncle Charlie said, "That was a fabulous victory for El Monte. They get to keep the thirty-twenty trophy for one more year."

"It was a boss game," said Pete. "El Monte scored twenty-one points, and Rosemead scored seven."

"And the bad animals didn't rip us up!" said Gail.

We laughed all the way to the car for the ride home. When Uncle Charlie drove onto the street from the parking lot, we heard the Four Knights singing, "Oh Happy Day."

Our high school's win over their rival school makes it a happy day. But how long will this happy day last when our town is plagued by burglars? Is the mysterious driver of the black Chevy pickup involved in those burglaries? Are we safe from him?

"Oh Happy Day," sang the Four Knights.

8

Knott's Berry Farm

Foggy fingers rolled around us as Hawk drove to Knott's Berry Farm in Buena Park, California. The car's headlights cut a shining path through the murky, gray clouds that rested on the road. From the radio, Frank Sinatra crooned his song, "A Foggy Day."

"It's funny that Frank Sinatra is singing a fog song," I whispered to Pete.

"What's funny is that Hawk has to listen to Mom and Dad's favorite radio station," Pete whispered. "It's almost noon. I hope we get to Knott's before the fog lifts."

"In the Bible, Job 26:8 says, 'He binds up the waters in his thick clouds,'" I said very quietly.

"That sounds like fog," said Pete. "Our teacher said that fog is like a cloud of steam over a boiling kettle. Outside, that misty air looks like steam, but its called fog."

"So the steam from my kettle is like fog," said Pete's mom from the front seat.

"Dad, tell him to stop," said thirteen-year-old Mary Jane. "His fog talk is crazy."

"Settle down, Mary Jane," said Pete's dad in a kind voice. "Pete's sharing valuable weather information with us that we all need to know."

"Thanks, Dad," said Pete. "Sorry, Sis. I'll try not to share when

■ 81 ■

FEROCIOUS FALL

you're around." Mary Jane *harumped* as Hawk drove his car into the Knott's Berry Farm parking lot.

"We're here," said Hawk as he parked. "Knott's Berry Farm is the most." As we climbed out of the car, a San Francisco Cable Car went *ding, ding, ding,* while it circled the parking lot then picked up and unloaded passengers at its station.

"Let's hurry over to Ghost Town to see the fog creeping around those old wooden buildings," said Pete as streams of sunshine battled the last wisps of fog.

"It looks like your fog is fading away like a disappearing magic trick," I said as it lifted. "Today, we escaped into the sunshine from foggy, wild weather."

Pete's mom said, "Pete, before you take off like a rocket, meet us at 6:00 p.m. in front of Mrs. Knott's Chicken Dinner Restaurant. Here's some money . . . have fun."

Off we scurried to have fun. As we passed Mrs. Knott's Chicken Dinner Restaurant on our left, I said, "I'm sure glad Mrs. Cordelia Knott started selling yummy chicken dinners at her berry farm over thirty years ago. I can't wait to have one later today."

"I'm glad, too," said Pete. "Her dinners got so popular that Mr. Knott built Ghost Town, so the people waiting in line to eat would have something fun to do. They could shop, watch the twelve-foot volcano blow its stack, or visit the old western buildings. Walter Knott moved them here from run-down ghost towns all around the southwest."

As we hurried towards Ghost Town, I pushed back my red cowboy hat and said, "With our store-bought jeans and cowboy hats, we fit right into Mr. Knott's western town. Oh, don't let me forget, I have to meet my cousins from Long Beach at the Covered Wagon Camp for their special square-dance recital at four o'clock."

"Okay, as long as I don't have to dance," said Pete with a warning in his voice and his eyes.

"You won't," I said. *Unless one of the dancers doesn't show up,* I thought.

We passed the Farm Market and turned onto Gold Mine Road. We stopped to stare down into the rocky pit called the Gold Mine. A volcano on the far corner hissed with a *roar, whoosh, poof.* The folks below us looked up then went back to panning for real gold with the help of several old prospectors.

"I panned for gold the last time we were here," said Pete. "That donkey down there turns the wheel to keep the water flowing for *all* the gold prospectors."

"I panned there, too," I said, "and took home a teeny, tiny tube of sparkly gold."

"Cool," said Pete as he waved me towards Main Street that ran through the heart of Ghost Town. "Let's go look at The Wagon Train Diorama inside The Gold Trail Hotel. Mr. Knott moved the hotel here board by board. It was the first building in Ghost Town."

"Sure," I said as I followed Pete through the hotel's door. I whispered, "I love this painting of Mr. Knott's pioneer grandparents as they traveled in their covered wagon across that hostile-looking desert."

"I dig the cowboys on their horses riding beside the wagons to keep them safe," said Pete. "That desert around the wagons does look hostile. So do those giant mountains in the distance. Pioneers had a rough ride."

Back outside, Pete went to drink from a fountain encased in rock while I wandered over to a bench with two statues sitting on it. I sat down between the rough-looking carved men and said, "Hi, Handsome Brady and Whiskey Bill. How are you?"

"The minute we get to Ghost Town you sit down with those two guys," said Pete as he jumped onto the wooden porch while still wiping his wet mouth.

"I know," I said. "I've been visiting these guys since the first time Dad brought me to Knott's Berry Farm when I was four-years-old. I had my picture taken with them."

"Later, gator," said Pete to my *friends* as we split up Main Street.

"Speaking of gators, do you remember our field trip this Friday, October twenty eighth?" I asked.

"Yeah, I can't wait to go to the California Alligator Farm that's across the street from here," said Pete. "That's gonna be boss."

I don't know about boss, but it should be interesting, I thought as we clumped on the wooden sidewalk next to a row of old buildings. We peeked inside Wing Lee Laundry and listened to the wood statue of Hop Wing Lee sing songs in Chinese. In the Sheriff's Office, four life-sized, wooden men played poker. A bearded wooden man in the Assay Office counted out an ore sample.

"Let's go peek in the jail to see Sad EYE Joe," said Pete as he traveled on the dusty street, walked behind Goldie's Place, and peeked inside the jail. "Joe looks so real."

"This old Ghost Town Jail smells real, too," I said as I sniffed like my puppy would at a stale smell.

"I hope the bullies at our school don't end up in jail like Joe," said Pete. "I'm glad Mr. Knott built Ghost Town so visitors would learn about America's heritage."

Back on Main Street, several ladies passed by dressed in long, hoop-skirted dresses. The town sheriff nodded to us. Across the street, Chief Red Feather posed for pictures as he stood between the General Merchandise Store and the Post Office.

Fall leaves crunched then swished under our tennis shoes as we turned onto Stage Road. The cloudless sky looked like a big, blue bowl over our heads. A breeze riffled my bangs. On Stage Road, we ducked into the Blacksmith Shop and Livery Stable. The blacksmith's fire flamed up as he pounded metal into horseshoes for the stagecoach horses.

On School Road, visitors like us watched the Ghost Town characters strolling around. "They wear costumes all year long and not just for Halloween," I said. "Let's go see the Old Red School House next to the Bird Cage Theatre."

"Okay," said Pete, "as long as I don't have to watch a melodrama."

"You don't have to," I answered. "But you know how much fun it is to cheer for the hero and hiss at the villain. The bullies at our school act like villains in a melodrama."

"They sure do," agreed Pete. "Whoever is burglarizing businesses around good old El Monte is a villain, too. I hope our El Monte law enforcers will catch him or them."

"Here in the old west, where the sheriff watches everything, it's easy to believe the villains will get their just rewards like old Joe. I'm inspired by being here," I said.

"That's cool, Carol Ann," said Pete as he stepped into the Old Red School House. The teacher, dressed in her "school marm" clothes, wrote words on the blackboard. Pete sat at a desk. He said, "I bet it was illuminating to learn in a one room schoolhouse."

"In a one-room school, the teacher would spot bullies right away," I whispered.

"And she would tell their parents," said Pete, "like we did." *Whoo, whoo, whoo,* whistled a train in the distance. Pete ducked onto the floor.

"It's not a duck and cover drill, Pete," I said as I stifled a laugh. "Look outside at Steam Engine No. 41 from the Rio Grande and Southern railroad line chugging along over there. The steam rising out of its stack looks like wispy, white clouds."

"Okay, so I'm overly prepared for a disaster," he laughed as he got up and brushed off his jeans. "Let's go over to Calico Square and ride that train." We scurried up School Road. "Can we stop in the Gun Shop to see their handmade bows and arrows?"

FEROCIOUS FALL

"Okay, if we can stop at the Candy Store," I said as we entered the Gun Shop.

Back out on the porch, Pete said, "I wish I'd had a bow and arrow set like one I just saw in there when I went to Gold Arrow Camp last summer. But I still had fun without it."

I laughed as I said, "You have fun no matter where you are."

"So let's go have fun in the Candy Store after we stop at Boot Hill," said Pete. "I like to stand on that grave with the beating heart and check out the real headstones."

"You *would* think Boot Hill is fun . . . you and thousands of other visitors," I said with a grimace.

After visiting the Boot Hill bunch, we bought hot dogs for lunch, plus candy and ice cream cones in the shops across from the Calico Saloon. Pete slurped his ice cream as we waited in line at the Ghost Town Station. When Engine 41 puffed into the station, on its narrow gauge track, we followed the leader into an orange-painted passenger car.

"I got dibs on that seat over there," I said to Pete. We sat down on real train seats. The conductor punched holes in our tickets as the train chugged forward and "cut out." It whistled its *whoo, whoo, whoo,* but this time Pete didn't duck and cover.

"This train ride is really cookin," said Pete as he waved.

Outside, on the platform, Chief Blue Eagle waved back. A welcome breeze blew my hair. The train chugged by the Burro Ride and the Haunted Shack on our right. Good old Boot Hill sat on our left, but disappeared when the train circled behind rugged rock formations. A commotion grew louder and louder as boots with spurs pounded toward us.

Bang, bang, bang, fired a gun as two masked gunmen *rushed* into our railcar. Through his bandana a gunman said, "This is a holdup. Reach for the sky." We did what he said and reached for the ceiling. The gunmen waved their firearms then they split.

■ 86 ■

"That fractured me," laughed Pete. "And I wasn't scared. Someday, I might work here as a gunfighter. Or maybe I'll be the sheriff. But I don't want to be a dancer!"

"I like the sheriff idea. Then you'll be a good guy," I said as our train approached the station. "Let's go ride the burros next. Okay?" *So I won't worry about square dancing.*

As we crossed Calico Square, we heard a voice calling Pete's name. "Oh, Pete . . . eee," said Mary Jane's voice. "Snap a picture of us with these statues dressed in their can-can costumes." Pete strolled to the porch, took the camera, and snapped pictures of his two sisters.

"Where are you girls going next?" asked Pete. "You want to ride the burros?"

They nodded yes and followed us to the line for the Burro Ride tickets. "Are those beasts clean?" asked Mary Jane. "I don't want to get my new outfit dirty."

"They look clean enough," said Pete as he paid for our tickets. "You ride on a leather saddle on the burro's back. You shoulda' worn denim threads like ours."

"Every time I go on one of your adventures, I get goopy," she said as we moved forward in line. Finally, we stood next to our burros and waited.

Attendants, dressed like prospectors, lifted smiling youngsters onto each burro's back. They strapped and synched all of us on saddles. I smelled leather, sweaty burro hair, and something stinky from the pile on the ground.

I patted my burro's neck as the attendants lined us up into a pack train, and we trotted forward. Mary Jane rode a white burro. My tan and gray burro shuffled next to Pete's grayish-brown beast of burden. Mandy's gray burro brayed *eeyore, eeyore* as we swayed with each step. We crossed the railroad tracks and plodded through town.

■ 87 ■

As Pete rode up next to me he asked, "Is a burro the same as a donkey? Where did the name come from?"

"It is," I said as we slowly shuffled on the dusty road. "Burro is a Spanish word. The Spaniards brought burros to North America. They're smaller than horses."

"Are they stubborn like cartoon burros?" asked Pete while swatting at pesky flies.

"Burros act stubborn sometimes, but they're mostly gentle, smart, and really curious," I said as our burros tramped along the scenic trail. My curious burro twitched his long ears.

"I can't wait for this ride to be over," complained Mary Jane. "I'm so bored."

"Well, Sis, check out the scenery behind the scenes," said Pete.

"I want to *make the scene* back where we started," she said and trotted forward.

Back at our starting point, we left our burros and scurried over to the Haunted Shack. As Mary Jane moved in front of us, I noticed brown stripes staining the back of her pink pants. *Yikes.* Pete noticed, too, and shushed me.

Mary Jane turned around and asked, "What's the holdup? Have you two ankle-biters got better scenery to look at than the *Haunted Shack?*"

"No, Sir, I mean, Ma'am," said Pete as we scooted forward in the ticket line behind the pink and brown striped scenery. "The front is clean, so don't tell her about her jail-bird backside."

In the holding area, we waited by a sign that said, PLEASE WAIT HERE FOR GUIDE. Soon, a guide ushered us through Slanty Sam and Shaky Sadie's abandoned home. Their haunted shack contained strange things inside of it: winding pathways, water running uphill, a pipeless faucet, and a room that defied gravity.

"Ha, ha, ha," laughed Pete outside of the scary shack. "I love that gravity thing."

"Ha, ha, ha," I laughed, too, so I wouldn't laugh at Mary Jane's pants.

We followed Mary Jane past Pet Land, the Seal Pool, and into Old MacDonald's Farm. "Mandy wants to ride the Mule-driven Merry-Go-Round," said Mary Jane. "Let's look at the barnyard animals in their pens as we go over to the ride. I want to avoid the ones who aren't in pens." She wrinkled her nose at some stinky smells. I did, too.

"Carol Ann, let's stop and watch Henny Penny play her piano for corn," said Pete. "Your neighbor, Mr. Chester, would love this chicken, and Buddy would love this barnyard."

"My little hound dog would sniff, bark, howl, and chase everything in here."

Hungry goats nibbled at Mary Jane's sweater sleeve until she shooed them away and hurried Mandy past the animal pens. The barnyard erupted into a noisy cacophony of sounds: *squeal, trill, snort, eeeeeyore, plop, stamp, peep, peep, peep, moo, honk, cluck, bark, baa, snort, whiney, plop, plop, plop.*

On the Merry-Go-Round swings, a mule moved us round and round and round. When the ride ended, we jumped off onto the ground. Mary Jane turned around to help Mandy and backed into some *plop, plop, plop,* from the mule. Now her brown shoes matched her brown striped pants. *Oops.*

"I can't believe it!" she screamed. "Every time I'm around you two something really *raunchy* happens to me. She stamped her brown, stinky shoes as she ticked off her grievances: Mr. Chester's chicken fiasco, go-cart grime, seagull . . . droppings, wormy fruit, putrid pumpkins, and now this hot stuff! It's your fault, and I'm telling Mom!"

As Mary Jane and Mandy scurried from the barnyard, Pete sang out, "Old MacDonald had a farm. E-I-E-I-O. And on his farm he had a mule. E-I-E-I-O. Here a *plop,* there a *plop,* everywhere a *plop, plop.* Gosh, Sis didn't have to have a cow because of a plop!"

We departed the farm and raced past the Seal Pool with its barking seals, across the Cable Car tracks, down the trail along Reflection Lake and the Indian Village on an island in the middle of it, past the Little Chapel by the Lake, past the Butterfield Stagecoach Depot, past the Bottle House, past the Coffee Shop, and through the entrance of the Covered Wagon Camp to watch the square dancing. *Whew! We made it!*

My Long Beach cousins, Pam and Sandy, waved us over to where they sat in the arena. The Wagonmasters, in their cowboy clothes, strummed their instruments while they sang, "Ghost Riders in the Sky." Pete and I sat down next to my cousins in some saved seats.

"We're up next," said Sandy. "I hope you like square dancing." Pete frowned and squirmed around next to Pam's puffy petticoat sticking out from under her costume.

When the cowboy crooning ended, the crowd clapped enthusiastically. My agitated Aunt Jean darted over to us and said with a frown, "Two dancers have dropped out, so you girls don't have a square. That means you won't be dancing." When she looked at us, her frown magically changed to a smile. "Hi, Kids, can you square dance?"

"We can't," said Pete in a voice that didn't dim the light in Aunt Jean's eyes.

Minutes later, after a quick lesson, a change for me from jeans into a frilly square-dance skirt, and a silent prayer, we joined my cousins' *square* on the dance floor in front of a thousand eager spectators.

"You owe me, Carol Ann," said Pete through clinched teeth as we waited for the music to start. "I hope I don't know anyone in that crazy crowd out there."

At least its shady under this giant, golden tree, I thought.

I smiled sweetly as the square-dance music began, and the caller gave us his instructions: "Bow to your partner," "Now join hands and do-se-do," "Promenade," "Circle left," "Now circle right," "Allamande," "Forward and back," and "Right and left Grand." We did a number of dance sequences, I changed back into my jeans, we said our goodbyes, and split.

Over at the Stagecoach Station I said, "You're a good sport, Pete." He swiped at his sweaty forehead. "And you *can* square dance!"

"No I can't," he argued. "My feet got mixed up. Those folks sitting around us on benches and in covered wagons eyeballed all my mistakes. I looked like a goof."

"They saw my mistakes, too," I said. "We both looked like goofs. I'm sorry you got dragged into square dancing," I said. "Do you forgive me?"

"I'll think about forgiving you while we ride on the stagecoach," he said.

On the Stagecoach Ride, we bounced up and down while it circled the park on its dusty route. The horses' harness' bells jingled and jangled a tune. Pete half-smiled when he lifted off the seat on a bump, but he kept his arms crossed. *Is Pete mad at me? Yikes!*

"Can we go visit the Little Chapel by the Lake?" I asked.

"Why not?" answered Pete in a grumpy voice as we exited the ride.

By the lake, we entered the small, adobe chapel, sat on a bench, and waited. Soon the lights dimmed, and a man's soft voice spoke words of inspiration and truth while soothing music played in the background. When the man's story ended, the curved-top doors in front of us opened automatically and revealed . . . a painting of a glowing Jesus!

In "The Transfiguration" painting by Paul von Klieben, Jesus seemed to step toward us out of the 1940 painting. His left hand covered his heart while he held his right hand out to us. His white, flowing robe with long, billowing sleeves glowed against a blue background. A heavenly light illuminated his peaceful, smiling face.

Pete's peaceful face whispered, "I'm not mad at you, Carol Ann."

"That's good," I said as we left the chapel and hurried back to Ghost Town. A stunning sunset of flame-colored clouds washed the western sky.

"I'm mad at myself for being a *brat* about helping your family," admitted Pete as we sprinted back along the trail past the Covered Wagon Camp. The square dancers had disappeared. The Wagonmasters now occupied the stage again and sang, "Tumbling Tumbleweeds."

"That's okay, 'cause we all act bratty at times," I laughed. "Right now we'd better act like a couple of tumbling tumbleweeds and scoot over to meet your folks for dinner."

Out in front of Mrs. Knott's Chicken Dinner Restaurant, Mary Jane impatiently tapped her brown-stained tennis shoe. "You're late," she complained and turned around to lead the way inside for a delicious chicken dinner. Her blonde curls bounced on her shoulders. Brown stripes still stained the back of her pink pants.

After the meal and some souvenir shopping inside Virginia's Gift Shop, Pete and I went with Hawk back to his car for the ride home. Pete's mom, Mary Jane, and Mandy still shopped while we waited. I twirled my beaded Indian bracelet around my wrist.

Pete said, "I've got my western souvenir tucked into my pocket." He patted his stomach and said, "That was the best chicken dinner ever! I'm full of chicken, mashed potatoes with gravy, green beans, biscuits, and boysenberry pie with ice cream."

"Me too," I agreed. "It was yummy. We had a blast today! Thanks for the invite."

"No sweat," said Pete as we waited outside his brother's car for the rest of his family. "Except for the square dancing, we had a boss time at the old farm today. And we learned a bunch about fighting bad guys and bullies."

"Like the Ghost Town Sheriff, we need to follow the trail of the bad guys and keep saving clues to help the police in our town," I said.

"Okay, Carol Ann," said Pete. "Keep collecting clues to catch the bad guys."

"We'll follow their trail like a good lawman . . . and lawgirl. I hope the bad guys who are burglarizing El Monte get caught before they catch us," I said with a shiver.

"They'll get caught," said Pete. "And we'll have a happy ending just like they do here in good old Knott's Berry Farm after a day of fun."

From inside Hawk's Ride, Frank Sinatra crooned, "Be Happy," and we were happy as we slipped into Hawk's car for our last ride of the day . . . our ride home.

But back at home, can we find a way to stay away from Rex and Neil even though we see them at school everyday?

9

Gravel Gertie's Flood

Rock 'n' roll music vibrated throughout Dan's Diner as we scooted out of the red vinyl booth and crossed the black and white checkerboard floor. Uncle Charlie led the way past the mushroom-shaped barstools lined up along the counter. Dan waved goodbye from his kitchen opening. In the back corner, teens danced near the jukebox.

The tune, "Whatcha Gonna Do?" by Bill Haley and His Comets, blasted around the diner. Pete waved to Hawk and his friends sitting on chrome chairs at one of Dan's round, chrome tables. Rex, Stu, and his brother, Barrett, sat at a neighboring table. Rex looked over at us and frowned while Stu smiled and waved.

Hawk asked Pete, "Are you going home with Dr. Charles?"

"Yeah, we're cutting out of here so we can take a drive through the gravel pits before dark," said Pete. "Dr. Charles likes to shake us up in his tank."

Rex must have overheard their conversation as he leaned over to us and said, "Watch out for trouble out in those pits. Don't get stuck."

"We won't," said Pete as we waved goodbye and paraded out the door into the cold night air.

Out in the parking lot, I stooped down behind Hawk's Ride and retrieved a shiny hook. I shoved it into my pocket before

Pete could see it. *Yikes. Is Hawk involved in the burglaries?* We passed Ernie's '32. His black Ford Hi-Boy sat next to several cool cars. Buddy appeared in the rolled down window of Uncle Charlie's tank. My little hound dog yelped a "hello" in dog language as we climbed into the car.

In the back seat, Buddy's excited tail wagged as he wiggled against us. "Hi there, little guy," I said as I picked him up so he could lick my face. "Were you a good boy while we ate dinner in the diner, and you ate your dinner out here?" Only crumbs remained of Buddy's dinner.

From behind the steering wheel, Uncle Charlie asked, "Are you Kiddos ready to shake up those chocolate shakes we had for dinner? Shall we hunt for Gravel Gertie?"

"Sure," shouted the little kids. Pete and I nodded our heads.

"Hey, Buddy, did you protect the car from burglars while we were gone?" asked Pete as Uncle Charlie started his car's engine, put it in gear, and drove out of the parking lot. "Ole' Man River," by Jimmy Ricks and the Ravens, played on the car's radio.

I elbowed Pete as we passed a black Chevy pickup. "Look at that truck, Pete," I said. "It looks like the truck we saw at the game Friday night. And we've both seen it on our street. The driver must be hanging out inside Dan's Diner."

"One of these days, we'll see him up close," said Pete. "We still don't have enough evidence to know for sure if he's the one burglarizing El Monte."

"Let's watch out for him and his pickup truck while we collect clues," I said as rain sprinkles hit the Plymouth's windshield. They disappeared when the windshield wipers swooshed them away. I patted the hook in my pocket. *Is this evidence against Hawk?*

"It looks like rain, Kids. It might not be a good idea to drive through the gravel pit tonight," said Uncle Charlie. "We can go another time."

"Not another time," said Little Charlie. "We want to search tonight!"

The other kids echoed Cousin Charlie. "Let's go tonight!" they chanted as the rain stopped hitting the windshield.

"We never seen Gravelly Gertie," said Gail. "Is she scary?"

"No one's *ever* seen Miss Gertie," said Pete. "She hangs out in the gravel pit and lives there in an old shack. She won't hurt us." Pete turned to me and winked.

"Since the rain has stopped, we'll take a chance," said Uncle Charlie as he turned onto La Madera Avenue and drove down the street. He passed by our houses, kept driving to the street's end, and onto a gravel road leading into the sand and gravel pit.

I glanced out of the window at the dark, cloud-filled sky and whispered to Pete, "This might not be a good idea. What if it starts pouring down rain in a crazy cloudburst like we had the first of the month? We'll get flooded down in the gravel pit."

"Oh, don't be a worrywart, Carol Ann," said Pete. Buddy woofed in agreement.

"Okay, I'll think about my Bible verses, so I won't worry," I said. "At least the rain will clear away all the smog we had yesterday. My eyes burned all day like campfires."

"The smog was so bad yesterday it was hard to see through it. Mom read about it in the newspaper this morning," said Pete. "It said that October twenty-fourth was a Smog Red day."

"My dad said he had a hard time seeing when he drove to work yesterday morning 'cause the smog was so thick," I said. "A rainy day will clear it away."

"Good rhyme, Carol Ann," said Pete. "The other thing in the newspaper, besides the football game results, was an article about the Boy Scout Carnival last weekend. It said one thousand Boy Scouts attended the District Carnival. The carnival was a blast."

"Your booth was really cool, too," I said. "My family liked seeing *all* the craft booths and watching the cowboy who did rope tricks."

Right then, Uncle Charlie's black Plymouth car surged up and over a bump like a roller coaster. We sailed to the ceiling and then down again onto the seat. Up and down we flew as my uncle negotiated the dirt haul road. The little kids giggled as they bounced. Buddy gripped the seat with his paws while wagging his tail.

In the distance, gray and pink clouds dotted the western sky as the tank rose up a hill and drove across the top of it before plunging back into the pit. Ominous-looking, cumulous nimbus black clouds rippled in the sky over us. Sprinkles hit our windshield once again then turned into full-sized rain drops. *Yikes, we're on the far side of the pit.*

Uncle Charlie raced by a tin shack with clutter and equipment dumped around it. He said, "There's the old girl's shack. There's no light on, so Gravel Gertie must be gone."

"I'm scared of Gravelly Gertie," said Gail as she snuggled closer to me on the back seat. On the radio, Dean Martin sang, "I'd Cry Like a Baby."

"We're okay, Gail," I said. "We're not crybabies like in the song. Uncle Charlie knows his way out of here. I have a good Bible verse I can share with you. It says, 'but in every thing by prayer and supplication with thanksgiving let your requests be made known to God.' That verse helps me to not worry so much."

"Thanks, Carol Ann," said Gail as she looked up at me in the darkening car. "I'm asking God to keep Gravelly Gertie away from us so I can get home to Mommy."

"That's good, Gail," said Pete as the rain beat against the top of the car like a base drum. Uncle Charlie swerved around a few more corners then up and down again. Pete watched Uncle Charlie watch the road.

Outside the window, in the gathering darkness, the gravelly ground beside the car shifted and moved in rivulets of running water. The windshield wipers whipped back and forth like tom-toms. I patted Buddy's head as he slumped down at our feet. *Is Buddy scared?*

I pulled my notepad from my pocket and flipped pages for a weather Bible verse. I whispered into Pete's ear, "Listen to this verse from Ezekiel about flooding. 'There will be an overflowing shower, and ye, O great hailstones, shall fall; and the stormy wind shall rend it.' Do you think the rain and wind will tear down that shack back there?"

"Aw, it's not raining that hard, Carol Ann," whispered Pete. "And there isn't any flooding or hailstones."

Yet, I thought. *This worrywart needs a sound mind.*

The tank's headlights slashed through the pouring rain as my uncle negotiated the haul road to take us home. The car slowed to a crawl while Uncle Charlie crept up to a low place on the gravel road we had crossed a while ago. Water ran across the road like a raging river. My uncle stopped, gunned the engine, and punched it.

The car skittered across the running water toward the uphill road on the other side of the river . . . then stopped. The tank's tires spun with a grating noise and shot streams of muddy water against our windows. *We're stuck!* Buddy whimpered. *He must sense that something is terribly wrong.*

Uncle Charlie changed gears, looked back out of the rear window, and backed up a few inches only to get stuck again. I glanced out the window next to me and watched as muddy water descended on us like a flash flood.

"Don't worry, Carol Ann, your uncle's a good driver. He'll get us out of here," said Pete as Dean Martin crooned the song, "Mississippi Mud," from the car's radio. "Dr. Charles, once when my dad's car got stuck we gathered sticks and rocks to put in front of the tires. Should we do that?"

"That's a fabulous idea, Pete," said Uncle Charlie. "Let's get out of the car, Kids, and gather rocks and twigs. And let's hurry. No slowpokes."

We left the warm, dry car for the muddy road. Our feet sloshed in the water next to the trapped car. The deep part of the newly-formed river ran behind us.

"This is bad news, Carol Ann," said Pete in a low voice. "Your uncle got shot down as he tried to drive up this hill. We need to think fast and gather stuff even faster."

Freezing outside air blasted us as Buddy chased me to some sticks and round rocks. I gathered them in my skirt that doubled as an apron. Rain poured down on us as we dashed back and forth dropping our debris in front of the tank's tires.

When a good-sized pile had formed, Uncle Charlie slipped into his car after waving us away from it. I gripped the kids' hands and backed them up. Pete stayed near the open window on the car's side to help my uncle.

Gail said through chattering teeth, "I hear Gravelly Gertie coming to get us."

On the hillside, I heard the noise of gravel slicing, ripping, and roaring toward us. *O God, please help my uncle move his car,* I prayed. Buddy howled frantically at the scary sound. Even in the early evening gloom, I saw the water level creeping nearer and nearer.

"Stay by me, Buddy," I warned my puppy in a loud voice over the rumbling noise. "It will be okay, Kids. Uncle Charlie will get us out of here."

Pete turned his head to listen to the howling and the rumbling. He turned back to my uncle and shouted, "Time to punch it, Dr. Charles."

My uncle revved the engine and floored it. The back tires spun in the mud as the front tires caught on the rocky bed we had created. The Plymouth's engine roared and competed with the roaring sounds racing to get us. *Yikes!*

The trapped machine rocked back and forth, back and forth then shot from its muddy prison like a rocket. Hailstones pelted our heads as we darted to the car. Buddy scrambled through the open door ahead of us. Pete slammed the door shut, and Uncle Charlie peeled flat out and up the gravel-strewn road.

Marble-sized hail beat the car's hood like fists. I turned and glanced through the rear window in time to see a Gravel Gertie flood swoop down over the spot we had just left. "Whew," I said. "We split just in time!"

Pete looked back and said, "Like crazy, like wow! We made ourselves scarce. Dr. Charles, you *really* agitated the gravel back there. You saved us!"

"Thanks to your help, Son," said my uncle as he looked at us in his rearview mirror. "Let's go home and get some of Aunt Jeanne's cookies."

"That sounds like a boss idea," said Pete. "Wow, that flood reminds me of the book I'm reading about Davy Crockett. When he was a boy, a bad rainstorm caused the Nolichucky River to flood over its banks and wash away the Crockett cabin. Luckily, Davy and his family got out first."

"That almost happened to Uncle Charlie's car with us in it," I said.

The tank climbed the last bit of gravel road and emerged onto the asphalt of La Madera Avenue. We cruised past several houses, an intersection, and more houses. Then Uncle Charlie turned into our driveway and the safety of our homes.

Hailstones pelted us as we escaped from the car. We rushed past the porch light, through the back door, and into the warmth of Aunt Ruthie's kitchen. A plate full of bumpy-looking cookies sat on the kitchen table surrounded by mugs of steaming hot cocoa.

As we crowded around the table to enjoy our dessert, I asked, "Does anyone want to know the name of these cookies my mom made in honor of our trip to the pit?"

"Yeah, what are they called?" asked Pete with a full mouth. "They're unreal."

"They're called . . . Gravel Gertie's," I laughed and took a bite of the chunky cookie in my hand. "They're full of nuts, oats, miniature marshmallows, and chocolate candy bits. They look gravelly like the stuff out there in the pit that tried to bury us."

"Fabulous cookies," said Uncle Charlie as he left the kitchen.

"That's a fabulous name for these cookies. And we had a fabulous time outsmarting Gravel Gertie's ferocious flood," said Pete as he grabbed another cookie to munch.

"Thank God, he helped us escape one more wild weather event during this ferocious fall," I said and finished my cookie. I glanced in Pete's direction. *Should I show Pete the hook I found behind Hawk's Ride? Who dropped it there? Will God help me prove that Hawk isn't a thief?*

The California Alligator Farm

"The California Alligator Farm field trip today is gonna be so cool," said Pete as we walked up La Madera Avenue on our way to school.

"It will be fun and educational, too," I said while holding a rectangular box containing six dozen cookies. "Mom baked these chocolate chip cookies for our harvest party this morning before the field trip."

"Yum," said Pete. "My mom's dropping off delicious donuts and apple cider."

As we passed the Bailey's house, I noticed a rumpled paper sack across the road. "Get that paper sack over there, Pete," I said. "It may be more evidence. Mom read in the paper that thieves with guns robbed the pharmacy's cash registers on Wednesday night. They put the stolen cash into a paper sack."

"Dad read that, too," said Pete over his shoulder as he picked up the sack then raced back. "I'm putting it in your school bag."

It will join my other clues. "According to the U.S Weather Bureau, it's supposed to be sunny today when the sun shines through those low, spread-out stratus clouds above us," I said. "Did you hear about the teen at the high school who threatened

■ 103 ■

a fellow student with a knife?"

"Hawk told me about that and about a guy who assaulted a seventy-six-year-old man in broad daylight. The guy took the man's clothes with only thirty cents in a pocket," said Pete.

"Are all these crimes being done by the same people?" I asked. "Somebody tried to steal a safe, and they did steal S-hooks from a company. Then pharmacy employees were threatened by robbers with guns who took money from the pharmacy cash registers."

"I don't know, but I hope the police hurry and round up these bad news burglars and robbers like the sheriff at Knott's Berry Farm did. He put Sad EYE Joe, the horse thief, in jail."

"That was a blast last weekend at Knott's Berry Farm," I said. "We'll be across the street from it today at the California Alligator Farm. I'll listen for the train whistle."

Once we arrived in our classroom, I put the box of cookies on a counter while I surveyed our decorations. Red, orange, and yellow construction paper leaves surrounded autumn scenes on our bulletin boards. Paper pumpkin cutouts hung on twine draped around the room's perimeter. Our drawings of pumpkins, black cats, and fall scenery adorned the walls.

In the back of our classroom, an orange tablecloth draped the refreshment table. Mums, pumpkins, apples, and colorful leaves created a festive fall centerpiece. Trays of donuts, cupcakes, orange-frosted cut-out cookies, and apple slices covered the table next to jugs of apple cider. Folding chairs sat along the back wall for our visitors.

"Please help me put these cookies on a tray," I said to Pete.

"Okay, if I can sneak one," said Pete as he lifted the lid and took a cookie.

Back at my desk, I admired our teacher's desk decorated with pumpkins and fall leaves. Tall, dried cornstalks stood on each side of the blackboard where today's schedule had been written in chalk.

The California Alligator Farm

Under the date, Friday, October 28, 1955, was written:

Class Party 9:00 a.m. to 10:00 a.m.
Leave on bus for field trip at 10:30 a.m.
Arrive at the California Alligator Farm
between 11:30 a.m. and 12:00 p.m.
Orientation upon arrival.
Lunch at 12:30 p.m.
Free time to explore and learn until 4:00 p.m.
Ride bus back to school.

Mrs. Rose said, "Good morning, Class. I hope you're ready for lots of fun today." She wore a long-sleeved, beige shirt tucked into a dark brown skirt. Her sturdy, brown-leather shoes looked perfect for traipsing around the alligator farm.

Our visitors and field trip chaperones arrived and sat in seats at the back of the room. We served them snacks on paper napkins along with paper cups filled with apple cider. Then we assembled at the front of the room for a short song recital.

As Mrs. Rose directed us, we sang words from "Autumn Is a Painter," "Halloween Visitor," and "Harvest Fun." During the last song, I clearly heard Pete loudly singing, "What fun we have at harvest time, with golden grain we work all day."

After the visitors left, the chaperones guided our sixth grade class into the bus. The driver fired up his vehicle, and we cut out for the California Alligator Farm located in Buena Park. "This trip is a kick," I said to my friends. Becky, Susan, and Eileen agreed with me as the bus cruised along.

"Our class party was a bash," said Susan. "But seeing those reptiles today will be a bigger bash." We nodded our heads in agreement and chattered like chipmunks about the fun we planned to have today looking at creepy reptiles.

One hour later, the bus pulled up in front of the alligator farm. Mrs. Rose gave us words of instruction. "I know all my students will conduct themselves with courtesy and caution today. I will be circulating the farm if you need me. Or, you may contact any of our kind and helpful chaperones. Have fun while you listen, look, and learn."

Once through the entrance gate to the California Alligator Farm, we stopped as a group in front of an attendant. His jungle attire and pith helmet looked like Uncle Charlie's outdoor clothes. Jungle-like trees, bushes, and shrubs grew around us. In the distance, pools dotted the jungle landscape.

The attendant said, "Hello, Cherrylee Sixth-Graders. Welcome to the California Alligator Farm which had a humble beginning in Los Angeles in 1907. The farm was originally started by Francis Earnest Sr. and Joe 'Alligator' Campbell. Two years ago, the Earnest family moved the farm to this much larger location."

The attendant kept talking. "Alligators are one of the oldest creatures on the planet. The name *alligator* comes from the word *El Lagarto* which means the 'lizard.' That's what the Spanish Conquistadors called the large lizards with giant teeth that they saw when they marched across the New World. El Lagarto became ellegarto and eventually alligator."

He finished by saying, "This farm has five hundred alligators and crocodiles, five hundred snakes, and many other tropical creatures to observe. We supply alligators to the motion picture industry and have had many famous visitors here, including Albert Einstein."

A boy in our class whispered, "That's killer and impressive."

"Einstein is that smart professor with the jets . . . brains," said Pete in a low voice.

After the orientation, the girls and I ate lunch at picnic tables under palm trees. The palms swayed in the California breeze.

Shadows and sunshine dappled the ground around us. "Let's visit the snake house then let's buy nuts to feed the spider monkeys in their cages," I said as we threw away our trash and traveled to the nearest building.

Once inside the snake house, Becky said, "They've got a nice lizard and snake display, but I'm glad they're in glass cages and not slithering around on the floor."

"Me too," I said with a shiver. "Yikes, look over there!" We watched a boy from our class press his face up to the glass in front of a huge King Cobra snake. The snake struck at the glass causing the boy to fall backwards.

He got up and said, "That was cool even though I flinched and fell."

"That made me flinch, too," said Eileen. "Let's exit this snake place. I don't want to stay for the King Cobra Snake Charmer Show. We just saw enough of a show."

A stroll through a tropical forest brought us to the monkey cages. The cute, little spider monkeys swung from tree limb to tree limb. We bought bags of nuts and offered them to the monkeys from our outstretched hands which we put through the bars. The monkeys grabbed the nuts and fled to safety for a nut feast.

We left the monkey area and stopped at a grassy, fenced-in area where alligators guarded nests that measured three feet high by seven feet across. Piles of white alligator eggs nestled among the grass and plants in their nests. Their white shells looked like giant versions of hen's eggs from Mr. Chester's chicken farm.

"When we read about alligators in class, the encyclopedia said that female alligators lay fifty eggs at a time," I said. "Those moms must be waiting for their baby alligators to hatch from their shells."

"Let's go find some baby alligators," said Susan as she led the way.

Nearby and still in the jungle, we found a lagoon of fenced-in pools and grass crawling with thousands of baby alligators. Their nine-inch-long, olive-colored, yellow striped bodies slipped over and under each other in a wriggling mass.

"Lots of those poor baby alligators have missing feet and tails," I said. "If they live long enough, this sign says they'll grow a foot a year. The females can grow up to nine feet, while the males may grow as long as twelve feet and weigh four hundred and fifty pounds. These beasts from the Crocodilian family can live for fifty or sixty years."

"Well I wouldn't want to see one of *these* beasts outside of its fence," said Eileen.

We heard a commotion and hurried to see what was happening. An old man with a bamboo rake and garbage can entered a grassy area filled with assorted pools and hundreds of good-sized alligators and crocodiles. Their gray or dark, olive-green bodies lounged in the sun or swam mostly submerged in the pools. Only their eyes showed above the waterline.

The old man raked, cleaned, and talked to the gators in his strong European accent. Some brave beasts scrambled over each other and snapped at the old man's boots. *Yikes.* He ignored them like the other lazy, lounging gators that ignored him.

"Hey, Carol Ann," called Pete. "You wanna go see the alligator show? The gators climb up a ramp and slide down a slide that's kind of like the one at your house."

"Sure I do," I said and turned to my friends. "Are you girls ready for the show?"

"I want to watch this guy as he cleans up in there and tries not to lose a foot or hand to those prehistoric-looking monsters," said Susan. The other girls agreed with her.

"See ya later, alligator," I said with a smile and a wave.

The California Alligator Farm

Becky called after me, "After while, crocodile."

At the slide show, Pete and I watched a nine-foot-long, giant, green gator climb slowly up, up, up a ramp on his strong, stubby legs. When he got to the slide's top, he crawled slowly over it and slid snout-first down into a large pool. The great beast's belly flop sent water flying. The crowd around us roared and clapped.

"That was boss to see that big daddy gator climb up and go flat out down that slide," laughed Pete. "His gig fractured me . . . he's funny."

"He made me laugh, too," I said. "And as long as he stays in his pool behind the fence I'll laugh at him all day." We tramped away from the show lagoon and along another path in this predator's paradise.

"Sometimes the gators do escape," said Pete. "I read a sign that said when it rains really hard and the nearby reservoir floods, restless residents can wander into backyard pools. The farm has even had people try to steal the crocs and gators for fun."

My eyebrows rose up into my bangs as I answered Pete. "Stealing prehistoric beasts, that could bite off your hand for a snack doesn't sound like fun to me." I looked up at the blue sky overhead and said, "I'm glad the sun's out and there's no rain in today's forecast, so we don't have to worry about escaping monsters."

"What monsters are escaping?" asked a voice behind me. I turned to see Rex catching up to us. Neil and Stu trotted behind him like pets. "You mind if we walk with you? Are you the monsters that are trying to escape?"

Neil laughed as Pete stopped and said, "The monsters are behind fences, except for one who escaped out onto this walkway." Immediately, Rex got in Pete's face and raised a fist. Stu dashed over and grabbed Rex's hand.

"Pete made a joke," said Stu. "Let it go." The two boys faced each other until Rex backed up. Rex looked like a snarling,

■ 109 ■

sinister, angry alligator.

"That joke was funny, Pete," laughed Rex. "You're full of laughs." Rex motioned to Neil. "Let's split from these goofs. That includes you, Stu."

"Stu, I'm sorry," apologized Pete. "Rex did one put-down too many."

"Aw, that's okay," said Stu. "I like hanging out with you and Carol Ann. Let's watch the handlers feed the gators and crocs at the giant pit."

We proceeded over to a fence surrounded by spectators. We stepped into a space for three. I looked down into the pit. *Yikes.* Dozens of giant alligators, like the one in the slide show, and crocodiles, with their more narrow snouts, crawled over each other in a dizzy dance. Down there the brown water smelled as raunchy as a sewer. A putrid punch of scent reached my nose. *Yuk. This smells worse than Mr. Chester's chicken farm.*

"This is so hip," said Pete. "What a cool place! Hey, what's the handler holding?"

"Whole, raw chickens," I said at the same time as he threw those raw chickens into the pit for a ferocious feeding frenzy. *Snap, crunch, chomp, snap, snap, snap, crunch, crunch,* echoed loudly out of that hole in the ground. My stomach did a flip-flop like those roiling, rolling, ripping, flipping, flopping beasts down below us.

"Like crazy, like wow!" said Pete. Stu shook his head in agreement. "When we first made the scene, the gators down there were calm and subdued except for a few climbing over their pals. Now look at them."

I didn't want to look at them anymore. The crowd around us pushed inward to get a better view. The fence wobbled. I pushed back into the crowd but hands pushed me forward. My head and shoulders leaned over the leaning fence. *Will my feet follow them?*

■ 110 ■

Will the gators crunch me like a raw chicken?

Someone whispered, "You see any clues down in that pit, Carol Ann?"

A mighty beast below me climbed onto his buddies, crawled part way up the wall, and snapped at me. *O God, help me, please,* I prayed and backed away from the fence. I stumbled out of the crowd. *Who pushed me?*

Mrs. Rose and Rex stood a few feet away. I heard Rex say, "I didn't push anyone. You must have been dreaming or you need an eye exam."

Mrs. Rose answered, "That's enough, young man. I saw you pushing Carol Ann. I heard what you said to her. You're in serious trouble, Mister." Our teacher escorted Rex away on the sidewalk.

"What happened?" asked Pete who now stood beside me. "Where's Rex going?"

"He got caught trying to push me into that gator pit," I said. "But I think he may have fallen into a pit of his own making . . . a pit of trouble. Finally, a teacher saw him doing something hurtful. I was almost gator bait, but I'm glad Rex, the bully, got caught."

"Yeah, me too," said Stu. "I'm tired of getting pushed around by him. Thanks."

"You're welcome," I said as we followed our teacher past the pit, past the ostrich pen, past a giant tortoise, and out to the waiting bus for our ride home to El Monte.

Exhausted students sat on the bus like a pit full of tired alligators before their feeding frenzy. Rex sat next to Mrs. Rose with his back to us. *What is he thinking?*

I pulled my notepad from my pocket to add a few notes. I glanced back to see the California Alligator Farm sign fading into the distance and whispered, "See ya later, alligator."

"After while, crocodile," finished Pete with a smile and a wave goodbye.

How will Rex be punished for trying to push me over that horrible hole full of snapping, ferocious, putrid, prehistoric creatures? I shuddered then wondered. *Will he be punished for any other crimes? Will he punish me?*

11

Lightning Strike

VROOM, VROOM, VROOM, roared Hawk's Ride as it rumbled toward us. We moved from the driveway into the open garage to get out of the way. Hawk and Ernie climbed out of the hot rod and stepped around it to hand Tim his crutches.

Hawk looked in our direction and said, "Are you guys here to help decorate for my harvest party tomorrow night?"

"Sure, Hawk," said Pete. "We can help carry tables and chairs outside to the backyard." Pete looked up and shook his head. "But it looks like rain."

Dark cumulus nimbus clouds moved overhead. "It's supposed to rain this afternoon and then clear up," said Hawk. "We'd better wait until tomorrow after school to decorate. Tomorrow night is supposed to be mild with a full moon for you trick-or-treaters."

"Can we help with some stuff here in the garage?" asked Pete.

"The guys are here to help me put scary games together," said Hawk. "You two can get the decorations organized and ready for tomorrow."

"Let's move the tables and chairs over near the garage door, so they're easy to get to," I said as I scooted between piles of decorations: bags of fall leaves, bushel barrels of apples, cornstalks, pumpkins, hay bales, black and orange crepe paper, orange tablecloths, and paper goods. Buddy sniffed at everything like he was on a harvest-time hunt.

"Good idea," said Pete. "We'll put everything where it's handy and easy to get."

The song, "I Don't Care If the Sun Don't Shine," by Patty Paige, poured out of Hawk's transistor radio. The garage grew strangely dark as if it mimicked the song. I picked up two chairs and turned to the open garage door. Rex stood there staring in at me. *Yikes. No wonder things just got darker!* Buddy growled a deep, guttural sound.

Rex ignored Buddy as he asked, "What are you ankle-biters doing?"

"We're helping Hawk organize his party stuff," said Pete as he carried a table past Rex and Neil.

Rex stalked in my direction. Buddy growled once again then circled around by me. I held the chairs in front of me for protection. Rex glanced at Pete on the other side of the garage and said, "You got me in trouble Friday, Carol Ann. I'm frosted about that. To make amends, give me that little spiral notepad you've been writing in all month." He towered over me and snarled, "I want that notepad . . . now!"

"You want a table?" asked Pete as he pushed one towards Rex. "Carry it over there with those others." Pete turned to me, lifted his chin, and mouthed the words, "Don't worry about that bully. I'm watching him."

Now, Stu's brother, Barrett, stood in the opening with Mary Jane at his side. She looked up at the El Monte High School football hero and said, "Hey, Rex and Neil, Barrett's been looking for you. He needs to split."

Stu's tall, handsome brother raked his right hand through his blond hair and said, "Let's go, Guys. I got stuff to do. We'll be back tomorrow night for the party."

I watched Barrett, Rex, and Neil stroll up the driveway and said, "Rex and Neil are taking off with Barrett in his red truck. Are they friends?"

"Rex and Neil are bad news," said Pete. "I don't know why Stu's older brother hangs out with them. Maybe he's watching them like we are." Buddy howled a plaintive cry.

"Gail would say Barrett's going to get 'taminated' by them," I laughed. "By the way, the little kids want you to see the party decorations they set up in my aunt's living room."

"Let's go see them right now," said Pete as he led the way through the squeaky gate between our houses. "Are there any cookies at their party?"

"There should be," I answered, "along with candy and treats for Buddy." My puppy twirled around then did jump-ups. His black ears and white-tipped tail bounced in the air.

As we passed the chicken car, I thought about the chickens at the California Alligator Farm. Pete must have been thinking the same thing. He said, "Like wow, I'm glad the chickens in your chicken car don't live anywhere near the California Alligator Farm, or they'd be food for the gator feeding frenzy." Buddy looked up at Pete.

"It's okay, Buddy," I said. "You can't ever go to that gator farm, or *you'll* end up as the feed in the frenzy of those ferocious alligators and crocodiles." Buddy whimpered.

Raindrops pinged on the chicken car's windshield. Thunder rumbled far in the distance. "Time to duck inside out of the rain," said Pete as he made a dash for my aunt's back door.

At the door, I bent down to pat Buddy's head and said, "Stay out here, Buddy, and guard the door. Here's a treat." He crunched his treat with sharp, white teeth.

I shivered at Buddy's crunching noises. They sounded like giant gator teeth crunching their food. *Yikes.* Inside the kitchen, coffee brewed in the percolator on the counter and sent out a strong aroma. Kids' voices led us to the living room. We found them dressed in their Halloween costumes.

The little kids popped up from their game on the floor then jumped around in their costumes like multi-colored, bouncing balls. Gail said, "Look at our decuurations. Aren't they pretty?"

Pete and I glanced around the room to see the pretty *decuurations*. Orange, paper pumpkin cut-outs hung on string taped over the windows. Black and orange, twisted crepe paper crisscrossed the room over our heads. Drawings of stick figures in autumn scenes adorned the walls. One stick figure looked like Buddy.

"This looks like a really cool party, Kids," said Pete as he went to inspect their orange-draped card table with its pumpkin centerpiece and trays of cheese slices, pigs-in-a-blanket, chips, and cookies. Pete dipped his hand into a bowl of black and orange jelly beans. "It's a real bash."

The doorbell startled us when it buzzed. The kids in their cat, lion, bear, and zebra costumes ran to open the door. Mary Jane put down her pink umbrella and strolled in holding Mandy's hand. *Add Mandy Mouse to the crowd and we have a full-fledged zoo.*

Mary Jane looked around and said, "Nice party. Who decorated?"

"We did," said Gail. "Do you like our decuurations?" Gail the lion swept her paw around the room.

"Have a cookie, Sis," offered Pete, "now that you've made the scene. Stay awhile."

"No thanks," she said. "I can't stay, because Debbie's on her way over. Ta, ta, Kiddos. Enjoy your party, and don't let Carol Ann mess with your harvest décor." Mary Jane picked up her umbrella at the door, popped it open, and darted outside into the rain.

Before Gail closed the door, I heard music wafting through it from the radio in Hawk's Ride. The song, "Stormy Weather," by

The Four Freshman, described the day. Thunder boomed nearby after a flash of lightning. *The* Hit Parade *helps me recognize songs on the radio.*

Gail closed the front door and said, "Mary Jane just pooped open her pink umbrella and left us. Does that mean she's a party pooper?"

Pete laughed out loud and said, "It sure does. Mary Jane's pooped open, pink umbrella makes her a party pooper for not staying at your party."

The little kids looked at Pete, shrugged their shoulders, and played another game. I sat down on the fireplace hearth and munched one of Mom's frosted cookies. Pete sat across from me with a fistful of cookies and one in his mouth.

"What did Rex say to you in my garage?" he asked between bites.

"He wanted my notepad," I said as I pulled it from my pocket. I flipped it open to my page of clues. "I wrote about the articles in the newspaper this month, a note about the black Chevy pickup truck, Rex's remarks, who he hangs out with, and the physical evidence we've found."

"You're so hip, Carol Ann, to take notes all month. Dad's police friend is visiting us later. Do you want to give him your notes and evidence?" mumbled Pete as he crunched another cookie. Lightning flashed outside the picture window. The living room lamps flickered.

Little Charlie turned on his dad's radio. Frank Sinatra crooned his song, "Jeepers Creepers." The kids shot to their feet and danced around the living room to the sound. They even sang along. "Jeepers, creepers, where'd you get those peepers . . ."

Uncle Charlie passed through and said, "That's some fabulous dancing, Kiddos."

Pete waited for my answer about our evidence while thunder rumbled. The storm crept ever closer. *Will it bring a crazy cloud-*

burst? Do we need to worry about flooding? Do I turn in the hook I found behind Hawk's Ride?

"I'm ready to give the police my information if it will help find the bad guys. If Rex is involved, he may find a way to sneak into our house and steal my evidence. I feel like Nancy Drew in the mystery book I'm reading for school."

"You're just like Nancy Drew as you gather clues linked to crimes. Now that Rex got shot down in his attempt to get your notepad, he may try something else," said Pete. "But don't worry. What's that verse you read to me about fear and power?"

I flipped through my little, lined notepad to the Bibles verses I had written down from my uncle's concordance. "It's from Second Timothy 1:7. The verse says, 'For God hath not given us the spirit of fear; but of power, and of love, and of a sound mind.' That's a really cool verse for a worrywart like me and a duck and cover diver like you."

"I like the power part of that verse," said Pete with a smile as Frank Sinatra crooned another song called, "Don't Ever Be Afraid to Go Home." Pete tapped along with the tune. "Even good old Mr. Sinatra doesn't want you to be afraid!"

"I'm working on the fear thing," I said. "I've mostly conquered my fear of shots since last April's polio vaccine fright, and I've ridden in Bob's go-cart since our summer scare." I looked back down at my notes.

"Do you have any verses about bullies?" asked Pete.

"I have one from Psalm 7," I said as I flipped several pages. I read, "'O LORD my God, in thee do I put my trust: save me from all them that persecute me, and deliver me . . .' That's a great one." *Please, God, deliver us from Rex, and deliver Hawk from having anything to do with the bad guys.*

The lamps flickered once more as a lightning bolt flashed outside the front window. Seconds later we heard the rumble of thunder as the storm scooted overhead. I said, "Psalm 97:4 says 'His lightnings enlightened the world: the earth saw, and trembled.' That's the perfect verse for *this* storm."

Pete got up, grabbed more cookies, and bolted to the front door. "Now that you're armed with Bible verses, go home, get your umbrella, your evidence for the police, and meet me at my house. I'll check to see if Dad's friend got here yet." Pete opened the front door, pulled his jacket up over his head, and fearlessly sprinted into the storm.

Back in my aunt's kitchen, I went to the phone. *I know God gives me power from fear, but on dark, damp, lightning and thunder days I like to see Mom waiting on our front porch when I run home.* Granny Mary smiled at me as I dialed the phone number. Mom answered on the third ring.

"Hi, Mom," I said into the phone. "Can you please wait for me on the front porch? I'm . . . scared." I smiled as I hung up the phone. *Mom said she'll be on our porch in five minutes. Yea!*

As I stepped outside into the inky darkness, the back door slammed behind me and made me jump. Buddy greeted me with a wagging tail. Through the driving rain, I saw our lighted, empty porch in the distance. Lightning flashed and thunder boomed at the same time. *The worst of the storm is overhead.*

Is it safe to run home right now? Will I get struck by lightning? If I don't go home, will Rex break into my house and steal the evidence hidden in my nightstand? Will robbers hold Mom and Mark at gunpoint to get my evidence? I looked down at Buddy and said, "When you see Mom on the porch, we need to fly like rockets."

Buddy barked then growled with a deep, rumbling sound like thunder. Out of the darkness, a hand encircled my arm and pulled at me. Buddy paced and barked ferociously.

"Let go of me!" I screamed. "What do you want?"

Rex emerged into the light and snarled, "I want your precious notepad." He grabbed at my pocket. I heard the fabric rip. Thunder rumbled overhead and shook the carport so hard that Rex stumbled backwards and let go of my wrist. *Proverbs says, 'the wicked stumble in times of calamity.'* I thought. *Is it too dangerous to run or more dangerous to stay?*

Buddy snarled at something else hidden in the darkest corner of my aunt's porch. My precious puppy growled as he scampered back and forth like he had something cornered. *What is it?* Another ferocious flash of lightning revealed *something* dark and sinister with a ghoulish, monstrous, masked face.

"O God, help me, please," I whispered with chattering teeth. I backed up to the opposite corner of the carport. Buddy stayed between me and the monster. Rex stumbled over to the ghoul as rain pounded the roof like huge hammers. Another flash of lightning lit up the shadows. I watched the ghoul run his right hand through his blond hair.

The gate to Pete's house squeaked in the wind. From our front porch, Mom yelled, "Stay there, Carol Ann, it's too dangerous for you to run home!" *I can't stay here,* I thought, *but can I get away?* I looked at our house and made my choice.

"Yeah, Carol Ann, it's too dangerous to run home to Mommy," snarled Rex as another flash of lightning illuminated both ghouls moving towards me.

"Let's go, Buddy!" I yelled, and we rushed into the rain. It soaked me to the skin like a waterfall. *O God, help me to run fast . . . ' upon the wings of the wind.' That's a verse I wrote down from Psalms 104.* The sidewalk stretched in front of me like a white, slippery snake. My footsteps splashed and pounded the pavement as my heart pounded in my chest. Buddy's puppy feet pattered in front of me.

"Run faster, Buddy," I screamed as I heard a scuffle behind me. "Those monsters are after us!"

Is this how a football player feels when he runs for a touchdown? Can I make it to the goal posts . . . my home where Mom is standing on the lighted porch? SIZZLE, BOOOM, screamed the storm like a really loud and vicious voice. *Yikes. Something scary is chasing us, but I can't look back.*

My feet landed on the porch at the same time as a FEROCIOUS FLASH and SINISTER *SIZZLE* lit up the darkness behind me and beside me and over me and all around me. In that same instant, an explosive *BOOOM* propelled me into Mom's arms. Buddy yelped painfully as I plunged down into hot, deep darkness.

Hawk's Harvest Party

Someone knocked loudly on our front door with thunderous banging noises. Kathleen and Gail fought to answer it first. "I got it," said Kathleen as she wrenched open the door. "Hi, Pete. Are you here to see Carol Ann?"

"She's putting on her costume," said Gail.

"I'm here," I said as I stepped behind my sisters dressed in my homemade costume.

A crowd had gathered outside. Hawk and his friends, plus Pete, Mary Jane, and Mandy formed a circle around a black design etched into the concrete of our front porch. The design blazed out from its center like a black sun.

"That's where the lightning bolt struck Carol Ann's porch," said Pete as I stepped past the front door to join the teens and little kids. "Like crazy, like wow! Turn around so they can see your back where you almost got torched by a lightning bolt."

"I didn't get torched," I said as I lifted my red cape and twirled around so everyone could see my back. "The heat from the lightning bolt's blast felt like a furnace, but it didn't burn me. It exploded behind my heels and threw me into my mom's arms. We both fell through our open door onto the living room floor. I kinda got knocked out."

Buddy sniffed with his usual snuffling sound at the burnt spot.

"You're really cookin, Carol Ann," said Hawk. "You must be livin life well since you outran a lightning bolt. We saw it explode on the porch right behind you."

Pete said, "I'm just glad Carol Ann is *cookin* and not cooked. We watched Carol Ann sprint through the storm to her house while the police handcuffed Rex and Stu's brother, Barrett. We saw the lightning bolt that zigzagged after her. Then, *BOOM*, we witnessed a massive explosion that sent Carol Ann flying. I thought she was . . . a goner."

Gail chimed in, "Mommy is gonna make molasses cookies, and I get one."

"Me too," said Pete. "Will you share one with me, Gail?"

Gail nodded as Mary Jane said, "Let's go home, Mandy, and put on our Halloween costumes." She looked at me and said, "See you later at the party, Lightning Girl. You should add a bolt of lightning to your red cape." She turned and stalked away with Hawk and Ernie.

From across the yard, Hawk said, "Your "put-down" of Carol Ann was mean."

"Are you a wee bit *jealous* of Carol Ann?" asked Ernie before their voices faded.

Pete still stood on our porch looking at the frightening design singed there forever. He glanced up at me and said, "It *was* mean of her to say that about you. She's jealous because you outran a lightning bolt and lived through the strike to tell about it."

"I would gladly give up the experience of last night and let her have it," I said.

"Your Halloween threads look cool, but who are you?" asked Pete as he looked at my costume.

"I'm Little Red Riding Hood. Mom made the costume for me," I answered. "I have a basket to carry like Red does in the story."

"That's boss. So get ready to go trick-or-treating," said Pete. "I gotta go change into my lion tamer threads. Meet at my house, and don't forget to put Buddy's costume on him."

"I'll be right over with Buddy the lion," I said. "Remember the story of Red Riding Hood who had to fight off the wolf? He was a bully in the fairytale. I thought it would be a cool costume for me to wear since *I've* been fighting a wolf-like bully all month."

"That's funny," said Pete as he departed. "See ya later, alligator."

Back inside my house, I loosely wrapped a wide, gold-colored fringe around Buddy's neck and tied a gold pom-pom to his tail. *Now, we're ready for trick-or-treating and Hawk's Harvest Party.* I grabbed my basket and a pillowcase for collecting candy and headed out our front door. Buddy sniffed again at the burnt mark then trotted behind me.

Pete met us on his driveway. He wore his Mr. Lincoln top hat from last summer's July Fourth parade, a white shirt tucked into jeans, and his red KID COURAGEOUS cape from his little boy-hood. Pete untied the knot under his chin and handed his special cape to me.

"Let's trade," said Pete. "Both capes are red. A courageous girl like you should let everyone know you're a KID COURAGEOUS, Super Sleuth, Lightning Racer."

"I can't take your cape," I said. "Lion tamers are courageous, too."

"Yeah, but I'm a fake lion tamer while you're a *real* lightning racer," he said as he unfolded a white pillowcase for holding his candy.

I untied my red cape and switched with Pete. My plain cape sort of turned him into a lion tamer. "Buddy is your ferocious lion," I said as Buddy spun in a circle shaking his 'lion mane' and whipping his 'lion tail.' "You can't shake those off, Mr. Lion."

Buddy scurried after us as we crossed La Madera Avenue, hurried to Stu's front door, and knocked. He answered the door and stood there in a long, flowing garment of blue, coarse fabric. He held a burlap sack and two painted boards.

FEROCIOUS FALL

"Hi, Guys," said Stu as he stepped out his front door. "I wondered if you still wanted to go trick-or-treating with me after everything that happened last night. I'm sorry about Rex and my brother trying to hurt you, Carol Ann."

"It's not your fault, Stu," I said as we traveled down his driveway and up the driveway next door. "I'm sorry about your brother being involved."

Stu answered, "Rex and Barrett both confessed to the police about their part in the burglaries all over town. They admitted to being burglars but not robbers with guns. The police have a tip about those other crimes involving firearms."

"Is the teen with the Chevy truck involved?" asked Pete.

"Rex ratted on the rest of their gang, including the teen driving the Chevy pickup truck," said Stu. "His name is Al Axel. He parked at his girlfriend's house then sneaked through backyards to meet Rex and Barrett. They're going to serve time in jail or prison. Neil's lucky he wasn't part of their crime spree."

"When the police tow truck hauled the Chevy truck away this morning, I saw scrape marks on the open tailgate," I said. "I guess that teen tried to steal a safe, but it fell out of his vehicle."

Stu said, "I always thought my brother would "steal" a great football scholarship, instead Barrett was stealing all around town. And it's terrible that he involved my friend, Rex, who's my age and way younger than him. Barrett should have stuck to "stealing" footballs from rival teams."

"I'm sorry about both Rex and Barrett," said Pete. "But I'm not sorry we snuck through the storm into Carol Ann's yard last night. I'm not sorry we hid behind the chicken car and saw Rex and Barrett bully Carol Ann. I'm also not sorry that the police cuffed them. And I'm really not sorry we watched the lightning bolt that chased Carol Ann and exploded behind her."

"I'm happy you're okay, Carol Ann," said Stu. "I'm also glad

■ 126 ■

that Barrett and Rex didn't hurt you and that you survived the lightning bolt. That bolt would have been something to see!"

We dashed up and down driveways and sidewalks, knocked on front doors, and yelled "trick-or-treat." The homeowners gladly filled our "sacks" with candy so we wouldn't trick them. They didn't know that we never planned to trick anyone. Around the corner at Mr. Chester's scary, old house, we crept slowly up his dark walkway.

"Old man Chester might not give candy away," said Pete in a whisper.

"His porch light is on," I said. "And he has a carved pumpkin sitting there with a flickering candle in it to welcome trick-or-treaters. So let's knock on his door and find out."

"You're brave, Carol Ann," said Stu as Pete pounded on the door.

We scooted back and waited. Something scary shuffled inside the house. Suddenly, the door opened and light spilled onto the porch. Old Mr. Chester stood silhouetted in the doorway leaning on his crutch. He sniffed his beaky nose while his hooded eyes looked us over. *Yikes.*

Then . . . he smiled a crooked smile, and through crooked teeth he said, "Hi, Kids, you want a cookie? I made them myself." Mr. Chester held out a tray of cookies with one gnarled and spotted hand. "Take one."

We each took one of Mr. Chester's home-baked, chocolate cookies and bit into their crunchy crust. *Yum.* Pete gobbled his up, reached for a second one, and said, "Wow, Mr. Chester, you're a great cookie baker! Thanks for the terrific treat!"

"You're welcome," said Mr. Chester as he put down the cookie tray. He picked up something that looked like a cookie, bent down to Buddy, and said, "Here's a doggy treat for the pup." Buddy stood up on Mr. Chester's leg and nabbed the treat.

"Thank you, Mr. Chester, for the cookies and Buddy's treat," I

FEROCIOUS FALL

said. "He's a special little hound dog." Buddy barked gruffly then wagged his lion tail.

We waved goodbye as we left to finish trick-or-treating in our neighborhood. Buddy scampered ahead of us then wove in and out of our legs like a pest. He shook his lion mane some more, but couldn't shake it off. Our sacks of candy weighed us down, so we heaved them over our shoulders like Santa Claus.

The dusk turned to night. Then a huge harvest moon rose up into the clear, black sky like a giant, orange pumpkin. "Look up," I said as I pointed. "It's a full moon tonight. At least it's not raining like last night." I pulled Pete's KID COURAGEOUS cape around me against the nippy night air.

"That moon looks so boss up in the sky," said Pete as he wrapped *my* cape around himself. "It's getting cold. We've got enough candy, so let's split for my house."

Back at Pete's place, we stowed our candy inside his house. Then we took off for Pete's backyard to eyeball Hawk's harvest party. "Rock The Joint," by Bill Haley and His Comets, blared from the record player. Bales of hay surrounded a dance floor. Black and orange crepe paper and balloons draped from one giant tree to another.

The tiki torches from Hawk's summer Hawaiian party blazed around the edge of the yard. Their flames shed light on cornstalk bundles and piled up pumpkins. Round tables with orange tablecloths and harvest centerpieces sat beyond the dance floor. Pete motioned us to an empty table. Buddy sniffed the ground around the cornstalks.

Mary Jane pranced over to us dressed in a lovely Little Bo Peep costume. Blonde ringlets framed her face as they escaped from under a pink, lacy-edged bonnet. The white, pink, and blue striped hoop skirt on her dress waved back and forth like a bell. Buddy investigated it.

"What do you want, hound dog?" asked Mary Jane as Buddy circled her skirt. She shook her shepherd's crook at him. "Leave, Doggy." She turned and asked Stu, "Who are you?"

Stu held out his two boards painted with rows of words and said, "I'm Moses from the Bible, and these are my tablets with the Ten Commandments written on them. You wanna read them?"

Pete piped up, "Yeah, Sis, read the Ten Commandments out loud."

Mary Jane gave her brother the evil eye and said, "Some other time. I'm waiting for Debbie to finish trick-or-treating, so Ernie can bring her to the party. Ta-ta, Kids."

She turned around and strutted away. "Stay here, Buddy," I said to my overgrown puppy. He sat down next to me and watched Mary Jane's swaying skirt as she crossed the lawn. *Last summer Buddy chased a cat around under Mary Jane's Hawaiian skirt. Is he thinking about that chase?*

From his chair across the table, Stu said, "Thanks, Carol Ann, for telling me to read the story of David and Goliath in my mom's Bible. I read about David defeating Goliath, and it made me feel like I could stand up to Rex and Neil."

"You're welcome, Stu," I said. "I'm glad that story helped you. Lots of Bible stories can help us make wise decisions about things."

Pete said, "That's one of my favorite Bible stories, because the kid fights that big, bad bully and beats him . . . with God's help of course."

"I also read about Moses and decided it would be fun to be him for Halloween," said Stu.

"Your costume's hip," said Pete. Buddy woofed in agreement.

"The best thing about reading Mom's Bible is John 3:16," said Stu. "You told me to look it up, Carol Ann, and I did. It says, 'For God so loved the world, that he gave his only begotten Son, that whosoever believeth in him should not perish, but have everlasting life.' That's my favorite verse."

"I thought you'd like it," I said. "It's my favorite Bible verse, too."

With a smile Stu said, "When I visit Barrett, I'm sharing that verse with him."

A commotion started on the driveway. Two policemen advanced straight to our table. *Yikes.* Everyone moved to give them a wide path. Their uniforms looked like costumes, but they were real and so were their guns.

Pete greeted them. "Hi, Officers, are you looking for someone?"

"We want to thank the young lady who collected all the evidence that will send a gang of thieves to prison for a long time," said one of the policemen. "We've got several confessions, we arrested the driver of the black Chevy pickup and his friends, and we've searched their homes for stolen property."

"She's right here," said Pete. "Stand up, Carol Ann, and meet these officers."

I stood up and greeted the two policemen. They both shook my hand and thanked me for collecting clues and evidence that would help convict some crafty criminals. I waved goodbye to them as they moved away.

"It's cool that the Heat . . . I mean police . . . thanked you," said Pete.

"That *was* really cool," I said and Buddy agreed with a howl aimed at the moon. "I'm glad they could use my notes, that I ripped from my notepad, and the evidence we collected."

"Rock Around the Clock," by Bill Haley and His Comets, vibrated across the yard. On the dance floor, our surfer friends from Huntington Beach were dressed like cowboys. Cap, Ten Man, Full Bore, and Ruler danced with the cowgirls they brought to Hawk's party. Cap, who was the leader of their group, smiled at us and tipped his cowboy hat in a salute. Then he swirled a cute girl around to the beat of the music.

At the buffet table, Pete, Stu, and I checked on the food: hot dogs, potato chips, baked beans, salads, desserts, and bowls of candy. We piled our plates high with food and went back to our table to watch the dancers.

Butch and his pal, Davey Boy, who belonged to The Cruiser Car Club, waved at us from where they kneeled next to a water-filled tub of bobbing apples. Butch ducked his head down, splashed around, and lifted his face up with a red apple clutched between his teeth. His jellyroll hairdo dripped water down his leather jacket with The Cruiser's logo on it. Both boys seemed tough, but they were our friends.

"Look at Butch," I said to Pete. "Last summer we thought he was bad news. I'm glad he wasn't and that he's here tonight having a good time."

Pete looked at him and lifted his chin in greeting. "Butch made wise choices when his friend didn't. Sorry, Stu, about Barrett."

Stu said, "I'm sad about my brother, but *he* made bad choices and lost his chance to get a college football scholarship."

"Speaking of bad choices," said Pete. "Last night, Carol Ann was forced to make a bad choice to escape into a lightning storm. God gave her a second chance when that lightning bolt *didn't* hit her."

"That's for sure, and I won't do that again . . . unless I have no other choice. The good thing is we learned all month about making wise choices when dealing with weather like crazy cloudbursts, dust devil whirlwinds, Santa Ana winds, fog, smog, flash floods, and lightning storms."

Stu said, "We also learned about how to deal with bullies like Rex. We need to let an adult know when a bully bothers us and not try to deal with a bully on our own."

"I need to apologize to you, Pete," I said, "for thinking Hawk had something to do with the burglaries, because I found a stolen S hook behind Hawk's Ride. I just knew your brother had to be innocent."

"That's okay," said Pete. "The truth always wins out, and Hawk's a good guy."

Western square-dance tunes poured from the record player. Pete groaned as he said, "They're not square dancing, are they?"

"They are," I said. "You want to square dance, Mr. Lion Tamer?" I asked Pete. Buddy's beady, black eyes looked up at me from his spot next to my chair. He tipped his tan and white head. One black ear drooped down. Then he sniffed at the air.

Pete frowned at me, stuffed one of Mom's chocolate chip cookies in his mouth, and said, "I'd rather face another ferocious fall than dance another square dance."

Buddy crunched a dog treat under the table as I tapped my toe to the dance tune. I said, "I'm okay if you want to escape from square dancing."

"Thanks," said Pete. "I'm grateful for *all* square dancing escapes."

Dancers twirled to a western tune under the bright, full moon on this calm evening. Moonlight streamed down on Hawk's harvest party. A breeze shifted the treetops which swayed the black and orange balloons overhead. Falling leaves floated onto our orange tablecloth with its harvest centerpiece.

Thank you, God, for helping us this ferocious fall, I prayed. *'For God hath not given us a spirit of fear; but of power, and of love, and of a sound mind.' That's from Timothy 1:7.*

Pete said, "I'm glad you're okay, Carol Ann, and that we learned to make wise choices about weather stuff and about friends."

I looked at Pete and said, "I'm glad for the wise choices we made, too. But I'm really glad for *all* our escapes. I'm *really, really* glad for lightning escapes, and bully escapes, and most of all I'm glad for good friends and our wild weather escapes."

"Aw, gee, Carol Ann," said Pete as he munched the rest of his cookie. "Me too!"

Epilogue

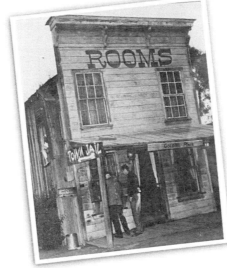

Goldie's Place-Ghost Town-Knotts Berry Farm

The wild weather in the San Gabriel Valley affected Pete and Carol Ann during the month of October, 1955. They learned about weather during their science classes at Cherrylee School. They learned to make wise choices about weather, too. While they dealt with weather situations, they also learned to deal with people situations as well.

Some of their classmates acted like wild weather. Rex's temper mimicked the whirling, roaring dust devil that chased Pete and Carol Ann on their school playground. The wisest choice in dealing with bullies was to let an adult know anytime a bully hurt someone with words or deeds.

While the wind whipped leaves off the trees and heavy rain cleared the smog from the air, Pete and Carol Ann collected clues about crimes taking place in El Monte. Their evidence helped stop a crime spree. Ferocious Fall was a time to listen, look, and learn. And the kids did.

Carol Ann Hartnell

HIKING Little Charlie, Carol Ann, Kathleen, Gail, and Cath on a hike to Sturtevant Falls

Gail and Carol Ann in front of their house

Carol Ann's house on La Madera Avenue

Carol Ann with chicken farm in background

Dad with Kathleen, Carol Ann, and Gail

Carol Ann on a bike next to Dad and Kathleen

re to Sturtevant Falls

ODGE JUNCTION

STURTEVANT FALLS

RY FLAT 1 1/2 MILES

P FAMILY

GHOST TOWN OR BUST

Dad with Aaron at
Knott's Berry Farm
in the 1960s

BUCKING BRONCO

SHERIFF

Dad & Aaron
at Knott's
Berry Farm

Kathleen & Carol Ann
sitting with Handsome
Brady and Whiskey Pete.

COVERED WAGON CAMP

KNOTT'S BERRY FARM

FOR MORE INFORMATION

Knott's Berry Farm
8039 Beach Boulevard, Buena Park, California 90620
(714) 220-5200   *www.knottsberryfarm.com*

Oak Glen, California
www.oakglen.com

Sturtevant Falls, California
www.sturtevantfalls.com

Gay's Lion Farm, El Monte, California 1925-1942
www.gayslionfarm.com

California Alligator Farm, Buena Park, California 1953-1984
www.californiaalligatorfarm.com

El Monte Historical Society and Museum/Donna Crippen
3150 Tyler Avenue, El Monte, California 91731
www.elmontehistoricalsociety.com

El Monte Chamber of Commerce
10501 Valley Boulevard, El Monte, California 91734-1866
www.elmontechamberofcommerce.com

Rosemead Library, County of Los Angeles Public Library
8800 Valley Boulevard, Rosemead, California 91770-1788
El Monte Herald newspaper on microfilm
www.rosemeadlibrary.com

How to deal with bullies?
www.dealingwithbullies.com

Hawk's Ride 1937 Ford
www.hawksride.com

Route 66 "Mother Road Museum
681 N. First Avenue, Barstow, California 92311
(760) 255-1890   *www.route66museum.org*

California Route 66 Museum
16825 South D Street, Victorville, California 92393-2151
(760) 951-0436   *www.califrt66museum.org*

■ 139 ■

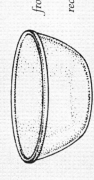

from the kitchen of Mrs. Jeanne Hartnell

recipe for Golden Lion Cookies/Gravel Gertie's*

ingredients

1 cup butter softened (2 sticks)
1 1/2 cups brown sugar
2 large eggs
1 teaspoon vanilla extract
1 1/4 cups all purpose flour
1 teaspoon baking soda
1/2 teaspoon ground cinnamon
1/2 teaspoon salt
3 cups quick or old-fashioned oats
1 2/3 cups Butterscotch flavored morsels

instructions

Heat the oven to 350 degrees. In a large bowl, combine butter, brown sugar, both eggs, and vanilla extract. Mix together until fluffy either by hand or with a mixer. Add flour (one cup at a time) baking soda, cinnamon, and salt. Mix well. Stir in oats and mix well. Then stir in butterscotch morsels and mix well. Drop rounded tablespoons of dough, two inches apart, onto ungreased cookie sheets. Bake for 8-10 minutes until golden brown. Remove from oven and cool on cookie sheets for 2 minutes. With a metal spatula, carefully move each cookie to a wire rack or place on a brown paper bag to cool completely. Makes 4 dozen delicious lion cookies.

*To make Gravel Gerties, follow above recipe but don't add butterscotch morsels and cinnamon. Instead add 1/2 cup chopped pecans or almonds, 1-2 cups semi-sweet chocolate morsels or chopped up chocolate candy bars.
                                                        Optional: miniature marshmallows

Glossary of 1950s Words

AFTER WHILE, CROCODILE: to say goodbye.

AGITATE THE GRAVEL: to leave/ to walk on the road.

ANKLE-BITER: a child.

APE or GO APE: to get really mad.

BAD NEWS: a depressing person/ someone who means trouble.

BASH: a great party.

BLAST: a good time.

BOSS: great.

BREAD: money

BUG: to bother someone.

BURN RUBBER: to accelerate very fast with a car.

CHERRY: an attractive-looking car.

CHROME-PLATED: a fancy car.

CLOUD 9: really happy or dreamy.

COOKIN': doing something well.

COOL: a long, drawn out word meaning someone or something extraordinary.

COOL IT: relax and settle down.

COOTIES: invisible infestations of the uncool.

CRUISIN FOR A BRUISIN: looking for trouble.

CUT OUT: to leave.

DIBS: to stake a claim to something.

DIG: to approve or understand.

DIG IN: to eat food.

DREAMLAND: a place to sleep.

EYEBALL: look around.

FEROCIOUS FALL

FAT CITY: a great thing or place.

FIRE UP: start your engine.

FLAT OUT: to go as fast as you can.

FLICK: a movie.

FLOOR IT: put a car's gas pedal to the floor.

FRACTURE: to amuse.

FROSTED: angry.

GERMSVILLE: a place full of germs.

GET WITH IT: to understand something.

GIG: work or a job.

GOOF: someone who makes mistakes.

GOOPY/ GROTTY: messy/ dirty.

HANG OUT: to be someplace.

HEAT: the police.

HIP: cool/ with it/ in the know.

HOPPED UP: a car modified for speed.

HORN: telephone.

HOTTIE: a very fast car.

ILLUMINATIONS: good ideas/ good thoughts.

IN ORBIT: to know something.

JELLYROLL: a hairdo.

JETS: to have brains/ smarts.

KICK: a fun or good thing.

LATER GATOR or SEE YA LATER, ALLIGATOR: to say goodbye.

LIKE CRAZY, LIKE WOW: really good and better than cool.

MACHINE: a car.

MADE IN THE SHADE: success is guaranteed.

MAKE THE SCENE: to attend an event.

MOST: high praise of someone.

NEST: a hairdo.

Glossary of 1950s Words

NOD: drift off to sleep.

NO SWEAT: not a problem.

ODDBALL: someone not normal/ uncool.

PAD: home/ room.

PAPER SHAKER: a cheerleader.

PARTY POOPER: no fun at all.

PILE UP Z'S: to get some sleep.

POP THE CLUTCH: to release a car's clutch fast.

POUND: beat up.

PUNCH IT: step on the car's gas pedal to go fast.

PUT DOWN: to say bad things about someone.

RATTLE YOUR CAGE: to get really upset.

ROCK: a diamond.

ROCKET: a fast car.

SCOLDED US ROYALLY: to get in trouble.

SCREAM: to go fast.

SCREAMER: a fast car.

SHOT DOWN: failed.

SIDES: vinyl music records.

SING: to tattle.

SOUNDS: music.

SOUPED UP: a car modified to go fast.

SPLIT: to leave.

STORE BOUGHT: bought from the store.

TANK: a large car driven by parents.

THINK FAST: said right before something is thrown.

THREADS: clothes.

UNCOOL: opposite of cool and not good.

UNREAL: hard to believe.

WHAT'S BUZZIN CUZZIN? : a question about what's happening.

The Adventures of Pete and Carol Ann continue with

WILD WINTER: Christmas, Clues, and Crooks

Pete said, "Some money is missing from our bake sale gig yesterday. Remember when I counted the money then put the cash box back under the table? Well, there's twenty dollars missing from the box! Someone dipped in there while our backs were turned when we cleaned up. Do you have your notepad handy? Let's write down some clues."

"That's terrible," I said as I pulled my notepad from my pocket. I flipped the notepad open to a clean sheet. "I'm ready. Tell me what to write."

"Write down that twenty dollars of bake sale money is missing from our sale on December tenth," said Pete. "And list the names of our helpers: Mary Jane, Neil, Angela, Adam, Edith, and an unknown crook or crooks."

I concentrated on listing the names and said, "But Buddy would have barked if crooks came up and snooped around our stuff."

"Some strangers did snoop around our stuff while you walked Buddy around the diner. They offered to help us. Did they help themselves to the twenty dollars?"

How many words can you spell from

OUR WILD WEATHER ESCAPES

1) _____
2) _____
3) _____
4) _____
5) _____
6) _____
7) _____
8) _____
9) _____
10) _____
11) _____
12) _____
13) _____
14) _____
15) _____
16) _____
17) _____
18) _____
19) _____
20) _____
21) _____
22) _____
23) _____
24) _____
25) _____

26) _____
27) _____
28) _____
29) _____
30) _____
31) _____
32) _____
33) _____
34) _____
35) _____
36) _____
37) _____
38) _____
39) _____
40) _____
41) _____
42) _____
43) _____
44) _____
45) _____
46) _____
47) _____
48) _____
49) _____
50) _____

Fall Word Scramble

Unscramble the following words:

1) EAEVSL   1) _ _ _ _ _ _
2) LLFA   2) _ _ _ _
3) IDNW   3) _ _ _ _
4) TREWAESS   4) _ _ _ _ _ _ _
5) LOOC CRAS   5) _ _ _ _ _ _ _ _
6) LBLATOOF MGESA 6) _ _ _ _ _ _ _ _ _ _ _ _ _
7) PALEPS   7) _ _ _ _ _ _
8) KUMPINSP   8) _ _ _ _ _ _ _ _
9) CHLOOS   9) _ _ _ _ _ _
10) KWEORMOH   10) _ _ _ _ _ _ _ _
11) DLOC   11) _ _ _ _
12) ERDSIAHY   12) _ _ _ _ _ _ _ _
13) ETSRE   13) _ _ _ _ _
14) SKHWADERI   14) _ _ _ _ _ _ _ _ _
15) AVHETSR EIMT   15) _ _ _ _ _ _ _ _ _ _ _

ANSWERS:
1) LEAVES
2) FALL
3) WIND
4) SWEATERS
5) COOL CARS
6) FOOTBALL GAMES
7) APPLES
8) PUMPKINS
9) SCHOOL
10) HOMEWORK
11) COLD
12) HAYRIDES
13) TREES
14) HAWKSRIDE
15) HARVEST TIME

150

Fifties Facts for October 1955

1) On October 3, 1955, Captain Kangaroo and Mickey Mouse Club premiered on television.

2) The Brooklyn Dodgers won their first ever World Series baseball game against the New York Yankees on October 4, 1955.

3) The "Cattle Call" by Eddie Arnold was the #1 song on the Country and Western Music Chart.

4) Students celebrated Columbus Day on October 12, 1955.

5) 1/2 gallon of milk sold for an average price of 44 cents.

6) Billboard's top song on October 14, 1955 was "Yellow Rose of Texas".

7) Busy Moms baked lots of oatmeal cookies and wrapped them in wax paper for student lunchpails.

8) A brand new T.V. show, Fury, premiered October 15, 1955.

9) Families picked apples and bought pumpkins at their local apple orchards.

10) President Eisenhower was recovering from a heart attack.

11) The movie, Rebel Without a Cause, was released on October 26, 1955.

12) The TV program, Father Knows Best, played every Wednesday night on NBC at 8:30 P.M.

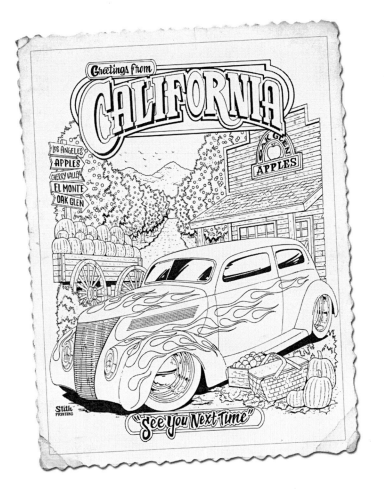

*"For God hath not given us a spirit of fear;
but of power, and of love, and of a sound mind."*

II TIMOTHY 1:7

Carol A. Hartnell and her husband live in the Southwest. They are blessed with four grown children and twelve grandchildren.
Visit the author at: www.cahartnell.com